PILLBOX 17

PILLBOX 17

THE STORY OF
A COMRADESHIP-IN-ARMS

By

KARL BRÖGER

Germany's Labour Poet

With an Autobiographical
Foreword specially written
for the English edition

Translation by
OAKLEY WILLIAMS

THORNTON BUTTERWORTH LIMITED
15 BEDFORD STREET, LONDON, W.C. 2

First Published - • • • 1930

TO ALL COMRADES-IN-ARMS
OF THEN, OF TO-DAY AND OF TO-MORROW

Let me be weighed in an even balance that God may know mine integrity.

BOOK OF JOB—6, xxxi.

CONTENTS

AN AUTOBIOGRAPHICAL FOREWORD

SPECIALLY WRITTEN FOR THE ENGLISH EDITION

I WAS born in the good old city of Nürnberg on March 10, 1886. Until I was ten years old March 9 was always held to be my birthday, but for some inscrutable reason the competent Registrar begrudged me this one day. So, I am one of those rare people, who, since their introduction into this the best of all possible worlds, consistently and persistently remain four and twenty hours younger than they really are.

My parents had nothing and were nothing, and therefore were not in a position to lavish anything on me beyond my three Christian names: Johann Karl Christian, with which I am in law still encumbered. When other people are talking about their childhood, I always listen to them with amazement. For I am passionately fond of fairy tales. I personally have no knowledge of childhood. Some particularly malignant hereditament always rises afresh in my gorge and leaves me marvelling even to this day to find that heart rhymes with smart and kiss with bliss. For what purpose will always remain shrouded in mystery for me. I betrayed myself even at school as an incorrigible rhymster, and at the age of seven had my first thrashing for this vicious propensity. It did not subsequently prove to be the only thrashing, even if in the meantime the others ceased to be administered by my father's belt, for he was a very precise and estimable man, but strong of arm.

Until I was twenty I let things take their own course. School occasioned me no trouble and, in the Secondary School, from which I was fired in the course of my fourth year, I excited no small stir by my craft for dissolving history into dates. After having done with school, life knocked me about according to my deserts. I was apprenticed to a trade, but cut rather too lavish a figure for a salary of 35 marks a month. I had to pay the penalty for it later on, when as maid of all work I had to do any job that I could not shirk in time. I was a builders' navvy, acquired merit in connection with relaying of the cables of my native town, worked in some lead works and nickel-coated the cast-iron parts in a stove factory. I achieved a total of 51 jobs in the course of six months, a record of which I used to be, if not inordinately, at any rate moderately proud.

Then Father State, whose unedified attention I had attracted on several occasions, took me by the scruff of the neck. I became a soldier and served my two years as a Bavarian infantry man in the delightful hamlet, Eichstätt. During this period I drew twopence halfpenny a day, and once even had the luck to scrounge a postal order for three shillings from home. How that came about the Lord alone knows. But by September 1908, a rather different type of individual emerged from under the military grindstone. They had knocked the frills out of me pretty thoroughly and no one, myself least of all, had occasion to regret it. Shortly after my discharge my mania for deducing smart from heart and bliss from kiss, became public property. The late Dr. Franz Muncker, Professor of Literary History of Munich University, attested it. So I was "discovered" as a "Labour Poet". Anyone who cares to know more about this phase of my life, will find it in my autobiographical novel, *The Hero in the Shade.**

My qualifications as a trained soldier in-

* *Der Held im Schatten.* Jena: Eugen Diederich.

volved me in the Great War. I was mobilized as a militia man in the 7th Company of the 6th Bavarian Reserve Regiment, and was wounded in the early fighting for the Loretto heights. I can still see the First Aid label through the second buttonhole (from the top) of my tunic; its single red edge indicated urgent treatment. The French splinter was embedded in the back of my head, but had been considerate enough to give the artery a miss. In any case the wound was serious enough to put me out of action. I spent the rest of the war, as no doubt every sentient and thinking human being, whether at home or on active service, spent it, in realizing it to be the greatest disaster that has ever overtaken the human race. My most noteworthy feat of arms lies in the fact that throughout my whole course of active service I did not fire a single shot from my rifle, model 98. That was not due to any deliberate intention on my part. In action I was a runner orderly, constantly in the front line, but I was not allowed to fire because my functions were those of a postman rather than of a rifleman. The number of times I missed being shot is evidence that Heaven had a purpose in view for me.

14

Up to date I have written sixteen books. May whatever else I have had in print as a journalist, as I have been since 1910, pass into limbo. We are all sinners one with another. The calendar now impeaches me of forty-four years and I cannot, I am sorry to say, rebut the indictment. I am still living in my paternal city of Nürnberg and have at times a feeling that it is a step-father of a town. But I prefer to keep my gift of prophecy a secret between ourselves. I am living with my wife and four children (my best collected works) in a jolly little house on to the roof of which I can climb without any undue effort. And what, if any, are my recreations or hobbies? I confess to an enthusiastic partiality for Bavarian beer and for shoes on the American model, and can be put to flight by gents lounge suitings and acquaintances I cannot avoid.

What the future may bring forth is, I am glad to say, not within my cognizance. So far as one can foresee things will remain "all quiet" not only on the Western, but on all other fronts.

KARL BRÖGER.

¶ Of Rengersreuth, of Pillbox 17, and of a Meal under Difficulties

RENGERSREUTH has not hitherto played a very conspicuous part in history. With its twenty-seven householders and one hundred and thirty fully accounted souls, not including the four-legged, it would have been a bit of a miracle if it had.

People in Rengersreuth are no better and no worse than elsewhere. They sweat a bit more than they laugh, and the red holidays in their calendar are in a strong minority as compared with the black workdays.

Otherwise, Rengersreuth lies prettily embedded between low hills in a narrow funnel of a valley down which a stream splashes in a hurry. Its idyllic situation is commended by the many trippers handsomely enough. They come in hordes from the big town near by to consume sandwiches, when they are not sausage rolls by way of a change, against Nature's heart in Rengersreuth. The native born are less ecstatic. It does, too, make all the difference whether you are gushing admiration for a hill at its foot or have to haul a load of muck up the self same ascent.

But when the glad sun is shining over Rengersreuth in its most cheerful mood and is making the red roofs beam on the landscape, the harassed little peasant farmer feels a glow under his cotton shirt, stiff with sweat in any case. He beams as well and feels that after all he is better off here than anywhere else in the whole cross-grained world.

Corporal Alois Schmalz stood astraddle at the observation slit of the cement strong point and gazed over the terrain. As far as he could see, flats—nothing but flats, dead level as a newly-planed plank and about as diverting.

Only here and there a shy eyot of undergrowth, looking as disconsolate as if it were conscious of its own disturbing existence.

The last trails of morning mist were still shrouding the sparse undergrowth and swaying in the faint morning breeze. The sun shot an arrow slantwise into the landscape and drew up the shadows noiselessly.

Something reddish gleamed on the far left. Alois Schmalz, to his astonishment, discovered that it was the glint of a red roof. Through his field glasses he made out the house pertaining to the red roof. It was in a state of almost complete preservation.

The corporal's eyes were tightly glued to his glasses. Schmalz could not get away from the roof and growled half aloud into his fantastic wartime beard, that displayed all shades of colour between black and green.

" Damme—a red roof—just as at home."

The glasses dropped slowly to his knee. The corporal fell abrooding. When had he last seen the red roofs of Rengersreuth? Was there such a place as Rengersreuth at all? If so, it must be somewhere in the moon.

A savage oath escaped him. Alois Schmalz turned away from the observation slit, aimed a blow at a fleeting rat, and closed his ruminations with the enigmatic exclamation :

" Swine of a pitch."

His voice, at no time attuned to whispers, rumbled like a growl in the cramped cement strong point, lying, four paces long by three broad, in an obstinate twilight.

A harsh voice came in answer from out of the twilight:

"Very true. . . . Have great pleasure in seconding the motion."

Lance-Corporal Hiesinger of the Army Medical Service, was squatting in the twilight in front of a candle. He had taken off his tunic and was examining his shirt for undesirable tenants that pay no rent. The candle-light flickered over his bared torso and now and then lit up Hiesinger's deeply lined face. The lance-corporal was tracing the seams of shirt and tunic with a needle and scoring the success of the pursuit, stroke by stroke, in pencil on the plank bed.

"Number 87. . . . I'm going to score a century to-day."

He stretched his hand over the candle and a slight fizzle immediately afterwards revealed that another louse had burst.

"The dam things are going to eat me up yet. . . . Worst of all are those with the Iron Cross on their backsides . . . wonder who conferred it on 'em?"

After that question addressed to an unknown fate, Hiesinger rose from the plank bed, cleared his throat and nose handsomely,

and yawned from one ear to the other. Then
—*pfoi! pfoi!*—he spat on both hands and
buried them in his tousled mop of hair that in
its turn had once known better days. For hair-
dressers, if only for business reasons, study the
care of the hair.

The strong point had gradually grown light
enough to allow its bowels, in outline at any
rate, to become visible. In addition to Schmalz
and Hiesinger, two more men made up the
garrison. One half of it at this very moment
rolled noisily from the upper bunk, sprawled
on to the floor and croaked half awake like a
bloated frog.

"Hullo, Scharf. . . . Drunken old sot.
Slept it off at last. The burying party might
carry you out asleep. . . ."

Machine-gunner Ernest Scharf blinked in
rather a bad temper at Hiesinger, rubbed his
bleary eyes and snarled with a ridiculously
high caterwauling voice:

"Chuck it, aspirin merchant. . . . My
sleeping don't do you any harm. . . ."

A bespectacled face emerged from between
two amunition boxes.

"Ah, our pillbox infant. . . . Had a
pleasant night, Mr. Artist?"

Volunteer Kurt Biegler first adjusted his spectacles before he gazed at the loquacious Hiesinger with wondrously quiet, child-like eyes. He was holding something that looked like a genuine towel in his hand and was peering all round the pillbox, looking for something.

"Spit into the air, Professorkin, and then stand under it. That'll give you a classy douche. . . . What a chap! . . . Wants water for washing! . . . Why don't you order champagne while you are about it?"

Corporal Schmalz gave the exigent artist a good-humoured thump.

"Our water's wanted for drinking. . . . You'll be unwashed often enough, Biegler. . . . Rub your eyes hard to make up for it. . . . You've got the first outpost go at the entrance. . . . Don't let me catch you making sketches and turning your nose earthwards —that damned airman's been hunting for our pillbox for the last five days. . . . If he spots us, not one of the lot of us'll want water or soap again. . . . They'll fan us into the trench grave without washing."

Hiesinger underlined every word of the

lecture with a peck of his pointed nose, and rubbed his abdomen significantly.

"Chaps, our little family party seems to be all present and correct . . . except for that loafer, Nuetzel . . . he ought to have been back an hour ago . . . where's our crater-water that the cook mistakes for coffee? . . . my belly's doing physical jerks. . . . There's something swinging about in my guts that beats any trapeze stunt. . . ."

Talking about being hungry only provokes greater hunger unless the stomach be well lined. Wherewithal it is lined is less important than gourmets believe. Even schnaps is a foodstuff if there is no better at hand.

Whether Machine-gunner Scharf followed this line of reasoning is not on record. What is on record is that he took a long and rapt drink from his water-bottle and to enhance its enjoyment, half closed his eyes as all experienced art connoisseurs do, and beautiful music is of redoubled charm for them therewith.

Good example has its effect in all places and at all times. Every man had his water-bottle at the ready in a moment and followed his mate's example in the spirit of comradeship. Even Biegler, the volunteer, took a pull, though the style of it was a little shame-faced and lacked soldierly dash.

"Biegler, turn out. . . . It's time you were on duty.   Leave that tin scuttle behind. . . . The service cap is more comfortable and, what's more, not so easy to spot. . . ."

Corporal Schmalz gave this order from the observation slit whither he had returned to duty. Biegler hitched on his pack and crawled out of the strong point on all fours.

Hiesinger was urging something on Schmalz in a low voice:

"I tell you Nuetzel has got hung up in the canteen. . . . Else he ought to have been back long ago. . . ."

A humming noise, dainty and distant, began to fill the strong point. This hum rapidly drew nearer and nearer and changed within a few minutes into a furious clatter.

"Gussie's coming. . . . Every man take cover. . . . Scharf, fetch in Biegler."

The corporal crouched down lower at the observation slit to keep the aeroplane in sight.

A giant hornet, the enemy flying machine, circled round the strong point, hardly sixty feet overhead, with an angry buzz. It was drawing its circles closer and closer.

24

Crash and rattle enough to make one's teeth scream. . . .

"The blighter's going to drop bombs . . . but one of these days, I'll get a line on him. . . ."

Corporal Schmalz stroked the water-jacket of the machine-gun and slid the barrel carefully through the sledge. The buzzing of the giant hornet died down again and dwindled to a vibrating lullaby.

"She'll be back within the hour. . . . Hope to God Nuetzel doesn't butt into her. . . . They let drive at every single unit. . . ."

Their faces were drawn tight round the temples. Grey-brownish furrows lined them, deep etched by a life that was only reeling out of death into death.

"Oughtn't someone to go out and bring him in? . . . I'll do it, if no one else will."

Hiesinger, talkative as ever, was on the point of opening his mouth. But on this occasion the corporal forestalled him. He laid his hand on Private Scharf's shoulder.

"You're a good chap, Scharf, and a champion ass as well. . . . Bring him in. . .? Why? For two people to be messed up in the

25

schemozzel and for me to be left here with a thick ear. . . . Furthermore, there're orders. Not a man to leave the strong point until relieved. And on top of that eleven o'clock chimes are going to start in a few minutes. . . . You know what that means, Scharf!"

When Machine-gunner Scharf was speaking, everyone looked round involuntarily to find the cat on whose tail someone was treading. That was what his voice sounded like, wherefore Scharf at all times preferred sleeping to talking.

"Eleven o'clock chimes. . . . Know all about that. . . . I've been up against it before now, Corporal. . . ."

"I know, Scharf . . . you're stout pals, you and Nuetzel. . . . So get on with it. . . . Because you're an old timer. . . . But only as far as the next crater. . . . Sixty yards half right and keep in touch, don't get out of sight. . . . I'll do trench picket myself. . . ."

The strong point was in the full glare of the forenoon sun. But at a distance of five paces it was hardly possible to distinguish it from its surroundings. The grey-brown block of cement nestled into just such another grey-brown undulation of the soil and did not rise a couple of feet above it. Behind the strong point a narrow communication trench, no broader than a slight man's shoulders, began. Private Scharf passed down this trench, keeping his head down. The N.C.O. leaned against the pleasantly warm wall of the strong point and waved his hand to Scharf. Scharf was just turning the bend and disappeared into the crater-field. In the entrance to the strong point, half in and half outside, Lance-Corporal Hiesinger of the Medical Service was sprawling on his stomach. He was drawing at a damp cigarette and spitting with practised skill at the bloated blue-bottles that, buzzing drowsily, were hovering round the entrance of the strong point.

"Going to be hot to-day before we're through . . . just the weather for Gussie. . . . He won't give us much peace to-day. . . . But it won't last long. . . . Sun's drawing too much moisture. . . ."

Never as a rule at a loss for an answer, Hiesinger, for the second time within the hour, missed his opportunity. The delicate hum, that had really never wholly died away since the first appearance of the aeroplane, increased in volume and drew nearer with amazing swiftness. It came from the opposite direction this time.

An arm shot up from the crater on the right and Schmalz, who was keeping the line of the arm under observation, saw a solitary grey figure hopping across the crater-field. Immediately afterwards the figure had disappeared again. On its heels, a machine-gun barked viciously. Machine-gunner Scharf turned the bend, out of breath.

"It's Nuetzel. . . . Gussie's on his track. Nuetzel's got the whole of our grub along with him."

Never did rabbit bolt more swiftly into its burrow than the Lance-Corporal of the Medical Service into the strong point. Corporal Schmalz knocked out his pipe first.

Again the machine gun barked.

Private Scharf was at the observation slit in a bound and was about to wrench their own machine gun round.

"Man, have you gone dotty? . . . The strong point must not be given away."

Scharf hesitated.

"But Nuetzel. . . . Is he to go West and our grub as well?"

There came a mocking clatter from without.

The hare and hounds game from crater to crater was in full cry.

"Turn out of the pillbox . . . we are going to occupy the communication trench . . . at the elbow in front of the crater, forty yards to the right. . . . Scharf to take the gun. . . . Biegler to bring up a box of ammunition."

With his steel helmet in his hand the N.C.O. was the first to creep out of the strong point, behind him Private Scharf with the machine-gun on his back, last, Biegler, who was clasping a box of ammunition tightly against himself, as if he were taking it out for a dance.

Bent double, the three men hurried through the narrow gully. At the bend, the N.C.O. threw himself down flat and beckoned to Scharf to join him.

A bare three hundred yards in front of them, but not sixty feet above their heads the plane was swooping, a hawk that has not quite decided on which side it had best strike its scared quarry.

Scharf had got the machine-gun into position. The corporal was squatting behind it, his finger on the button, his steel helmet half down the back of his neck.

"If the blighter would only turn. . . . I can't get him square. . . . Ah . . . at last!"

The machine-gun barked.

With a bound, as if about to take a fence, the plane rose almost vertically, swayed undecidedly, and then veered off sharp right.

Twice, three times came a bright flash from the under-carriage of the fuselage.

"Get back to cover. . . . Gussie's signalling . . . in five minutes we are going to have their heavy stuff about our ears."

Nuetzel, the ration fatigue, scurried across the open with two mess tins in either hand and a fifth fastened into his webbing belt. Perspiration was pouring down his face in streams.

With a quick grab, Private Scharf secured two tins and crawled backwards into the communication trench as quickly as might be.

Afar off from the other side came a dull thud. An almost soothing organ note was borne through the air that soon became an uncanny grinding roar and suddenly, close to the crater, a hundred yards to the left, a tree of whitish grey smoke sprouted from the earth.

"Take close cover and get back. . . . I'm taking charge of the gun."

With the N.C.O. bringing up the rear, they

worked their way back crab-wise. It was only fifty yards to the pillbox, but once inside, every man was panting with exertion and gasping for breath.

Outside, the daily bombardment had begun.

"Ouf! That was some steeplechase. Believe I've swallowed my Adam's apple. . . . Well, you gave her what for, Corporal . . . for the time being Gussie's gone home for repairs . . . for all I care she can hop it for keeps. . . ."

Private Nuetzel was a squat barrel of a man. A pair of merry pig's eyes twinkled in his honest face, otherwise undistinguished for manly beauty. A layer of mud half-an-inch thick covered his whole figure impartially from the soles of his feet to the roots of his hair.

"Damn it all . . . this time my number was all but up . . . the blighter gave me a damned good run for my money. . . . Into the crater. . . . Out of the crater. . . . The falling's soft enough there. . . . But the mud. . . . Not to mention the stink. . . . The very devil."

The sleeve of his coat wiped down his face and left a picturesque tracery of dirt and sweat.

"Couldn't tear yourself away from the canteen again, you old beer tub."

As a general rule, Nuetzel put up with a good deal from his friend Scharf, but now he turned on him:

"Canteen? . . . Damned lot of it—the rotten cooker was late in coming up again . . . ration issue was to be at seven o'clock—at half-past eight I began to make a stink and got the grub at last. . . . And to put the tin hat on it I must needs bump into Gussie . . . my dear chap . . . I deserve a fortnight's leave at least for that stunt . . . and then you roll up and talk rot."

The medicine man cut further discussion short.

"Chuck cackling . . . I'm hungry."

They were all hungry and therefore turned with one accord to the mess tins.

At this memorable moment the ways of Providence were once again made manifest. They are as wonderful and incalculable as the flight of a high velocity shell.

As Hiesinger was picking up his mess tin from the floor, it struck him as being suspiciously light. He raised the mess tin to the level of his eyes distrustfully. Then, holding it out rigidly at arm's length, he uttered a tragic howl.

"Empty. . . . Here's luck for you . . . and clean shot through . . . dirty work!"

The mess tin had, in fact, got a clean cut abdominal gun-shot wound.

"That bullet ought to be in Gussie's petrol tank not in my mess tin. . . . Such a handsome bit of kit as that was . . . for two years I've been lugging it about. . . . What lashings of grub I've had out of it, if in Roumania alone. . . . Chicken and dumplings are better than dried vegetables. . . . What's an infantryman without a mess tin to be after? . . . Swine of a pitch. . . . You found the right description for it a few minutes ago, Corporal."

This wail for his perforated mess tin would, with Hiesinger's proven gift of the gab, probably have gone on growing shriller and more heart rending. The N.C.O., however, cut the lamentation short.

"Damn the mess tin. . . Can't be helped. . . . There's enough to go round for five. . . . Come here and cut in."

The five of them squatted side by side with their mess tins between their legs on the floor, and ladled out a cold greyish-green mess.

c

"Barbed wire every other day. . . . And for grub of this sort I very nearly died a hero's death on the field of honour to-day. . . ."

Resentfully, Nuetzel forked his dried vegetables over, piled up a heaped spoonful, and was about to shoot the charge in his mouth:

"Hullo! . . . Shavings? . . . . Where does that sort of greengrocery grow?"

The discovery was passed from hand to hand for the expression of expert opinion. It was undoubtedly a shaving, neither unduly small nor unduly thin.

"Well, might be worse. . . . When I am feeding I always say to myself, open your mouth and shut your eyes. . . . That's the best way to deal with it. . . . They stewed a whole sack down once in our cooker . . . no one noticed it, nor did the sergeant, until the sack had been eaten. . . . If that were the worst we had to swallow. . . ."

The enlightened views of the Medical Service introduced a conversation on food in general and army rations in particular.

"I think it rotten that there should be two kinds of rations for officers and for other ranks. . . . I once copied out a poem . . . they had it painted up in the captain's dug-out."

34

Private Scharf rummaged laboriously in his tunic, and at length produced a notebook of doubtful cleanliness into the not overpowering light of the pillbox.

" It ought to be somewhere about here. . . . Here 'tis. . . . This is what they painted up in the O.C.'s dug-out:

> " *It ought to be the fashion*
> *To have one kind of ration:*
> *As 'tis, we quickly tire*
> *Of nothing but barbed wire.*

" That gave it him all right. . . . Eh? "
Nuetzel, too, had a notebook in his hand and was turning the pages eagerly.

" I wrote out a verse rather like that. . . . Listen :

> " *We feed just more or less,*
> *The orf'cers have a mess*
> *For us it would be sauce*
> *To have a second course.*

" Them's my sentiments to a T."
The conversation became more animated. It did not contain many expressions of commendation.

Outside, the bombardment went on.   At

regular intervals bursts thudded round the strong point. But not a single shell fell alarmingly near.

"So far they haven't spotted us. . . . A bit of luck that we are in the thick of the crater-field. . . . They can go on plastering that for the duration for all I care. . . . Who is on duty? Scharf? . . . Nuetzel relieves him. Carry on."

The N.C.O. threw himself full length on the plank bed. Biegler had seated himself at the observation slit and was working away, absorbed, at a pencil sketch.

Nuetzel and the Red Cross man put their heads together. The water-bottle passed from mouth to mouth and the corporal's snorts and snores accompanied a muffled duet. They had sunk their quarrel and were singing the lance's favourite song with feeling:

> *And another little drop,*
> *Another little drop,*
> *Won't do us any harm.*

¶ Thunder by Night.
¶ "But a Chap must have Luck."

TOWARDS evening the bombardment died down. Only as single spies did the shells howl past overhead.

The cloudless day passed away in a dull twilight that brooded hot and heavy, over the countryside. Crater and hollow were filled in by the early shadows. The scattered eyots of undergrowth stretched their straggling branches motionless to all quarters and looked piteously lost in the barren desolation of the terrain.

The strong point was still enshrouded in darkness. The atmosphere in the pillbox, what with smoke and reek, was thick enough to cut with a knife and lay heavy on heart and lungs.

"There's something in the air, Hiesinger—something not quite O.K. . . . We know the symptoms. . . . They haven't been firing much during the day. . . . If it'ud only come on to rain hard. . . ."

The N.C.O. turned up his collar.

"Don't mind me, Corporal. . . . Rain, on top of everything. . . . I don't want to drown in this monkey cage of cement. . . ."

Schmalz dug the Red Cross man in the ribs.

"Suppose you want to pick and choose, do you? . . . Suffocated or drowned. . . . Comes to the same thing in the long run. . . . But there's a reason why I want rain. . . . Why have they been firing so little to-day? . . . Eh? . . . Because they are pushing their batteries forward. . . . They always do that after two days of weather like this. . . . The craters are almost dried out to the bottom. . . . A good downpour and they'll be full to the brim . . . and then the artillery advance'll have the dirty end of the stick again and we shall be left alone. . . . Rain like that has saved the lives of hundreds before now. . . ."

The candles were sacrificing themselves to the vain effort of shedding light. At half an arm's length their power was spent.

But Machine-gunner Scharf could still be distinguished. He was lying on his stomach on the plank bed and conducting a curious concert, in the course of which he occasionally backfired and made the candle flicker.

"Look at Scharf. . . . Wonder if that chap will ever be done in. In it since the start . . . wounded four times . . . and always back in the front line. . . . I've known him now for over a year in our M.G. company . . . a first-class observer and marksman—I'm no better myself. . . . A prickly customer, of course . . . a chap who gets at him about saluting or drill'll have a tough job. . . . It is idiotic too, in the case of a man like Scharf. . . ."

The sleeper was groaning and talking in a muffled voice in his sleep:

"Do dig a bit quicker . . . else I shall suffocate. . . . Easy, easy. . . . Don't pull so hard. . . . My arm. . . . Very good, sir."

The rest of the dream monologue trailed off in unintelligible muttering.

"He has been buried before now . . . down on the Somme. . . . A man does not shake that sort of thing off easily."

The Red Cross man's eyes searched the N.C.O.'s face uneasily and roamed over the whole pillbox.

"Fact is, we're caught in the sweetest thing in the way of rat traps, Corporal. . . . If a

39

real crump lands on our roof, they won't have to bother about burying us. . . ."

Schmalz rubbed his cheek bone. It crackled like a display of miniature fireworks.

"Why think about it? . . . Another forty-eight hours and we're relieved. . . . Before you know where you are, time will be up."

Nuetzel slipped through the entrance.

The N.C.O. looked him sharply up and down.

"Anything the matter? . . . Anything happening outside?"

Nuetzel scratched his head behind his ears.

"Can't say exactly, Corporal. . . . Round that crater there, where I was sweating blood this afternoon, it struck me as suspicious. . . . Something clinked. . . . I saw a shadow, too. Is there a patrol of ours anywhere about?"

The brow of the strong point's commander was puckered.

"One of our patrols? . . . Not to my knowledge. . . . That's the direction of the H.Q. of the battle sector. . . . So in all probability it's runners. . . . In any case we'll have a look-see. . . . Nuetzel remains on

40

guard at the entrance. . . . Biegler accompanies me. . . . Hitch on a couple of crackers. . . . You never can tell. . . ."

Blue black night enveloped the pillbox, not too dark but of a stillness that forced all the blood back on to the heart. A solitary cricket was chirping unconcerned and made the stillness the more oppressive by its fiddling. Outside in the bend of the communication trench, flat on the ground, lay Schmalz and Biegler.

The sound of friction of metal on metal, then a muffled voice:

"Where's the blasted M.G. nest hiding? According to the map we ought to be running our noses into it about here. . . . This is the sort of fool job to give a fellow, mate. . . . But I'm not going stumbling about in the dark much longer. . . . I'll tell you that straight. . . ."

The two runners had a pretty severe shock when not three yards away from them on the right, the whispered, but abrupt and clear-cut challenge came out of the darkness:

"Halt! Who goes there?"

Two seconds sufficed to convert the encounter into a matter for general congratulation.

Nuetzel's vigilance had not been at fault. He could not, of course, know whence the nightly visitants of the craterfield had come or on what errand.

The corporal was holding the order close up against the uneasy flicker of a candle. Type-written and manifold, it read:

> " *To the Group commanders i/c Battle sector.*
>
> " *Extreme preparedness for action from 9.30 p.m. Enemy attack expected. Signal outposts to be doubled.*
>
> " *Call for barrage only in extreme emergency.*
>
> " *The posts will be evacuated only on express orders in writing.*"

On the margin was added in red pencil:

> " *Special orders for strong point 17.*
>
> " *Strong point 17 is a key position. It will be held to the last cartridge. Fire will only be opened on massed targets in front or half left.*
>
> " *Keep sharp look-out!*
>
> " *In the terrain in front of strong point 17, officer's patrol of ours.*

"Lieutenant Goebel and 6 O.Rs.

"Return of patrol looked for between 12.30 and 2 a.m.

"Order will be burnt forthwith after noting."

Full of thought, Schmalz thrust his finger between the middle buttons of his tunic and lugged out a watch of the pre-Flood era. The hands showed 10 p.m. precisely. The others crowded expectantly round the candle. Nuetzel and the lance-corporal had read the order simultaneously with the corporal over the latter's shoulder, and looked at one another with meaning.

"Aha! . . . Mission of signal honour. . . . Only wonder who's after the Iron Cross Class I in the back lines. . . . Tut, tut. . . . That wasn't meant for you, Corporal. . . . You've got it up already."

Schmalz looked the Lance firmly between the eyes. There was a quiet challenge in his gaze.

Holding the paper in the candle until it had been reduced to a dull grey ash, the N.C.O. was already giving his orders.

"That's that. . . . One way or the other,

43

we know what we are up against . . . the pillbox is going to be held. So far I have done every job as well as I knew how. . . . Hope that's you fellows' idea too. . . . Scharf and Biegler will take the first spell, Nuetzel and I will relieve. . . . We don't want light signals. . . . We are only five hundred yards from their front line. . . . We only open fire straight ahead or half left . . . and only on massed targets . . . anything going on the right or behind us, is not our pigeon. . . ."

The next two hours went by at snail's pace.

Schmalz, Hiesinger and Nuetzel sat on the lower bunk smoking for all they were worth and made the atmosphere, thick enough to cut as it was, by so much the denser.

Conversation dragged itself listlessly from word to word.

"This swindle's going to last for another ten years," asserted Nuetzel, as he filled his short pipe with some impossible weed. It smelt like a forest fire.

"Pardon me," interjected the Red Cross man. "By that time we shall be crawling about on all fours, provided we are able to crawl at all. . . . Everything has a tip where it comes to an end . . . the sausage only has

44

got two. . . . Silly ass you are. . . . In ten years' time I shall be walking about on my own beard. . . . As it is, it's growing out of my ears. . . ."

Hiesinger was exaggerating grossly. His growth of beard was pretty well the only thing about him that could be called reticent. In the first place his hair propagated on some mysterious scheme of its own; very thickly close round both ears, not at all under his nose and elsewhere at its own good pleasure, a tuft here and a tuft there. The man looked as if he had hung a pair of worn foot cloths, very much in need of washing, round his ears.

Nuetzel had decidedly greater pretensions to a beard. Without any line of demarcation the hair of his head continued and throve luxuriantly and mosslike on every spot appropriate to hirsute growth. That Nuetzel's snub nose still succeeded in emerging from this thicket was a bit of an achievement.

Not to speak of Schmalz. He had the trench beard proper; a tangle of hair looking like rusty barbed wire drawn criss-cross all over his face.

After glancing at the watch aforementioned, the N.C.O. nodded to Nuetzel.

" Time to relieve them, Nuetzel."

They slipped out of the pillbox one after the other, Schmalz leading.

After a whispered conference with Scharf, who had nothing of importance to report, the corporal propped himself against the cement wall and directed Nuetzel ten yards higher up the communication trench.

The night had become as black as pitch. There was not a star in the sky. A high wind was blowing in gusts from the West and piling up heavy clouds. Three paces in front of one's eyes, the crater zone was as good as walled off. It was only rarely that a Verey light went up. But every three minutes a wan spectral finger from the rear pointed into the terrain. The searchlight swept to and fro restlessly. Far away on the right, muzzle flashes showed up. It was only sporadic fire all the time and its effect lay well out of sight.

By the first hour after midnight the thunderstorm was fairly brewed. The West wind soughed heavily and rolls of thunder sounded nearer.

The advanced line became lively.

A Verey light rose out of the unknown depths of space, displayed, at what height or distance it was impossible to determine, its brilliant white bulb of light, and tore a sharp rent in the darkness.

A second, third and fourth floating light sprang into flower. Then a red rocket in headlong rage shot up into the night and let loose a wild crash and shriek which a more distant coughing and howling overpowered. In between, turning the bowels to water, yapped machine-gun fire, and the sharp, tearing detonation of bombs pierced the din.

As if they wanted to outbid the outbreak of the artificial thunderstorm, the skies, too, plunged into the riot. Lightnings flashed, thunder reverberated unending in their wake, and rain swished down, not in drops, not in torrents, but in whole clouds that only broke close above the ground.

The two storms raged in unison. The night, hitherto so silent, seethed in wild uproar.

Flattened against the pillbox wall, the corporal peered straight ahead of him. The swirl of rain splashed down on his steel helmet and ran, tepid and soaking, down his neck. After the sticky heat of the day this deluge from the skies was a refreshment.

In undiminished violence the thunderstorms

47

above and below raged and with every minute grew more violent.

Overhead the sky was one glow. Flashes and crashes increased in breadth and depth. Dozens of floating lights were in the air and drew yet more discharges out of the darkness. No longer a narrow strip, the whole front from one end to the other was ablaze and spitting blood and fire.

The heavy stuff passed overhead to the rear. In front of the pillbox—ten yards, maybe a hundred, away—trench mortars and field artillery traced a line of fire. Through the shrill tear of the bombs, machine-guns ticked with murderous monotony.

The corporal strained his eyes till they hurt. But no human sight could avail to pierce that wall of blackness and blinding rain.

" Looks like a raid in force? " the N.C.O. confided to his beard.

The German lines now began to show signs of liveliness. A white parachute light joined forces with another to a glaring double flare. This bulb stood for seconds above the pillbox and lit up the crater-field with its glare and an arm became visible, for no longer than it takes a man to open his eyes, against the streaming darkness. This arm was completing a forward swing.

An exploding bomb screamed.

German artillery opened fire. The shells shrieked on their way and fell so short that the ground all round the pillbox heaved.

Nuetzel stumbled out of the communication trench through the rain, plastered in mud from head to foot, softly swearing to himself.

"The damned fools . . . they're spraying our communication trench. . . ."

He gulped and spat with rage.

"They go and plant a mangel-wurzel—should say it was a twenty-one centimetre—straight in front of my nose. The trench is filled in for a good five yards. . . . No blighter can hold on over there. . . ."

Nuetzel pointed to the right.

In salvos of fours and eights the guns were pounding every square foot of the ground and churning the soil to powder.

Scharf crawled into the entrance.

"Your ground sheet, Corporal. Not that it'll be much good in this deluge. . . . Good Lord! . . . Swine of a pitch. . . ."

The N.C.O. shook himself and contributed more rain to the rain.

" Decent of you, Scharf . . . you've a head for everything. . . . The ground sheet's no damned good. . . . No more's the rain for the matter of that . . . . four and twenty hours too late. . . ."

Scharf crawled completely out of the pill-box.

" Bit thick, isn't it?   Playing some skittles."

He blinked at Nuetzel who was still swearing under his breath, but none the less persistently.

" What's the row, Scheps? . . ."

Scheps was Nuetzel's nickname and was meant to convey the idea of one who is just a little daft.

Now, Nuetzel was by no means weak-minded, except on one point; he was chockful of superstition and regarded it, for example, as a scientific fact the he could only be hit by a projectile that had been filled exactly at midnight.

But whether belief or superstition, human beings are all sensitive on this particular point.

Nuetzel, in any case was not one of the most sensitive of souls and rough-tongued people are, as a general rule, always ruder when they ought by rights to be asleep of nights.

50

"Scheps he calls me. . . . Scheps. . . . In
half a mo' I'll catch you a biff that'll bury you,
you silly-faced mongrel. . . ."

Nor was Scharf a man continent in speech
and one term of endearment led to another,
until the two fighting cocks were crowing at
each other with swollen combs.

"Ho, ho! Stow it, both of you," the corporal intervened. He had muffled himself up
in the ground sheet; snorted angrily under his
steel helmet and wrung out his water-logged
beard like a sponge.

"Just look at these silly goats! Standing
about in the open at half-past one at night, in
the rain, too, and blaming one another for
their strawberry marks . . . and there are our
own guns making mud pies of our communication trench."

The bombardment continued and became
even hotter. Two machine-guns spat and chat-
tered with outstanding zeal with the result that
the German artillery at last became aware of
them. The very next salvo was lifted a couple
of hundred yards further and seemed to have
found its billet, for the M.G.'s were abruptly
silent. Schmalz growled complacently.

"Those chaps have copped it . . . they

seem to have woken up behind, the slug-a-beds, and have given over mistaking our trench for the other chap's wire. . . ."

A vivid flash of lightning seared the sky and the crash that followed on its heels was such, that for a heart's beat all other noise was lost in the peal. At the same time the clouds spent themselves in a renewed deluge.

But this last outburst exhausted the violence of the thunderstorm. Thunder and lightning died away rapidly. Only the rain kept on persistently, even if it abated a little in density.

"Hush . . . just listen. . . . Someone coming."

The three men strained their ears into the darkness.

"That'll be our patrol . . . making its way back."

The tramp of feet was quite distinct by this time and with it, the low clink of metal.

"They're keeping too far to the right," whispered the N.C.O., and was out of the trench with a bound.

The retreating thunderstorm had relieved the inky blackness of the darkness. The night had become lighter. The clouds flaked apart and here and there allowed the glimpse of a star.

Schmalz had hardly made good his balance when the ground twenty yards in front of him burst. Once, and once again, a giant hand swept the man off the crater-field and hurled him backwards into the trench.

What had happened?

Had he duplicated himself or was he lying on himself? Tremendous pressure was taking his breath away.

The N.C.O. squared his shoulders and raised the upper part of his body.

Then laughter rose hot in him and broke forth.

The air pressure of a heavy shell had flung him backwards into the trench and a man of Goebel's patrol on top of him. He was listening to this remarkable incubus cursing lustily by his side.

"Damned swindle . . . . blasted weather, curse it. Keep your bloody feet to yourself, damn you. . . . You are kicking my whole counting house to pieces."

Schmalz was on his feet in one movement.

"Leg it, boys. . . . Get into the pillbox. . . . Else we are going to get it in the neck."

53

Thirty yards to the right a shell burst in the trench.

In the pillbox, Scharf patted the newcomer on the back roughly, but in friendly wise.

"What a go, mate! . . . A twenty-eight centimetre at least and not even the smallest return ticket to show for it. . . . I should like to deal at the same shop where you get your luck from. . . . It's the real stuff. . . ."

The man, thus welcomed, growled a curt invitation always proffered among the common people but never accepted, blew his nose and looked reproachfully at Schmalz.

His nose was bleeding and, with the rest of his face, bore marks of a kick or two.

The N.C.O. was holding his grandfather of a watch over the candle and was staring, lost in thought, at the dial.

It was 2.10 a.m.

¶ " Patrolling, you haven't got to. . . ."
¶ Rescue in the Night.

PRIVATE SCHRAMM of the officer's patrol under Lieutenant Goebel, reported.

" We were supposed to be relieved at four o'clock. . . . I don't think. . . . So we lay in a dug-out for the sixth day . . . not that there was much to grouse about in that . . . except for the lice and other livestock. . . . Yesterday when it was growing dark, the C.S.M. races through the lines and bawls for me among others. . . . I don't like hearing my name shouted aloud . . . specially not by our C.S.M. . . . Nothing good ever comes of it. . . . So I thinks, you go on shouting, and don't budge. . . . But what's got to be, has got to be. . . . The next jiffy he'd jumped me and I had got my whack of signal honour. . . . Under Lieutenant on reconnaissance. . . . If you have any luck you may break your finger picking your nose. . . ."

The speaker filled his lungs with cigarette smoke and tenderly stroked his proboscis.

" Ten sharp, we pushed off . . . Lieute-

nant and six O.R.'s . . . after five minutes of
it we were all sweating like bulls. . . . The
night was like a baker's oven stoked for overtime. . . . Well, we crawled about the country, a bit forward, a bit rearward, a bit to the
right and a bit to the left, with our noses to the
ground. . . . We didn't find any half dollars
. . . but at last, to make up for it, a triple line
of wire. . . . We stay lying in front of it,
staring our eyes out of our heads. . . . I'm
lying beside our officer. . . . He nudges me
in the ribs and moves half right. . . . We
wriggled on another twenty yards or so . . . .
and struck it . . . the gap in the wire, I
mean. . . . 'What about shoving your nose
a bit further into it,' thinks I, and caterpillars
my stomach another three feet forward. . . .
That tore it. . . . I don't think. . . . Our
C.S.M. on such like occasions always says:
'That's a situation' . . . and the blighter's
not so far wrong . . . . made me feel quite
muzzy. . . . I've been in a schemozzel or
two before now . . . but fair's fair: when
they are spraying you from three sides you
don't want another chap pouring water by the
bucket down the back of your neck until it
runs out of your boots. . . ."
56

At this point the representative of the Medical Service thought it proper to give tongue to his views:

"All because of a drop of rain. . . . You must be a very dry blighter."

Schramm, a sturdy, curly-headed man in his thirties, did not look the type of person unable to stand up for himself. He turned his head slowly in the direction of the Red Cross man and measured his interlocutor from top to toe. He incidentally noted that Hiesinger was as dry as a bone.

"Did he say dry. . . . Damned clever if you are fugging in a dug-out and let others do patrols in the open. . . . Don't talk through your hat, Court plasters. . . . You first of all put your nose. . . ."

It was not any consideration for conventional good manners that caused Schramm to leave the sentence unfinished. How thoughts develop and fade away in the brain is still a bit of an unsolved problem. Schramm turned away from the Red Cross man, tested his swollen nose again, and continued his report:

"Damn it all. . . . I had almost forgotten the most important thing. . . . My officer's out there still. . . . He stopped one. . . .

How and where? . . . Haven't the foggiest notion. . . . But I do know he's out there still. . . . Lieutenant Goebel's been my platoon officer for the last three months. . . . One of those small, white-faced chaps. . . . He's only an amateur at the game like the rest of us. . . . On the reserve, one of those autumn manœuvre hoppers. . . . But one of the sort a chap can get on with. . . . Doesn't shirk his job and doesn't pinch his men's rations. . . . I've got to bring him in. . . ."

Outside, the uproar was going on merrily. The heavens, it is true, were silent. They had had their fill of the competition in making a din and relinquished the effort and the honours in favour of the guns which were, to give them their due, making noise enough for three full-grown thunderstorms. Nuetzel had hitherto been squatting on an ammunition box in silence He got up now and moved towards Schramm.

"You are going to bring the officer in? . . . I'm with you. . . . I'm soaked through as it is to my ticket of admission to the trench grave . . . and a chap can't get more than soaked."

Hiesinger intervened. The Red Cross man

58

was unable to listen to any conversation for more than three minutes without intervening.

"What's that? A wounded man to be brought in. . . . Without me? Then what am I here for at all? . . . Shooting—that's your job. . . . But bringing in a man who's stopped a packet, that's up to me in the first place. . . . A locksmith doesn't take on cobbler's work. . . . And what does Nuetzel know about first aid? . . . My mess tin knows more about it and that's gone West. . . ."

This unforeseen and not to be foreseen switch to the mess tin caused general astonishment. It was only Nuetzel who felt the jab and reacted promptly.

"He keeps on bleating about his blasted dipper. . . . I'm glad that his feeding trough has got a hole through its tummy and not me. . . . If I want to lend a hand to fetch in the officer, that's got nothing to do with any beastly aspirin merchant. . . ."

The two hot heads glared their challenge at one another.

Corporal Schmalz curtly bade them come off it.

"Of course, we're going to look after our

own wounded. . . . There may be more of
them left outside than the officer. . . . How
we're going to set about it is up to me to decide.
Hiesinger's got most experience in a job of this
kind. . . . So he'll take the lead. . . . Schramm
knows the spot where the lieutenant is. . . .
He will proceed with Hiesinger. . . . I reckon
the spot to be about a hundred and fifty yards
straight ahead with a slight inclination towards
half right. . . ."

Schramm nodded lively approval of the
N.C.O.'s reckonings.

"Nuetzel will keep touch with you two.
. . . He knows his way about that crater from
what happened to him yesterday. . . . I am
going to be in the next crater, forty yards from
the trench. . . . Scharf will be on duty at the
pillbox and will keep his eyes as skinned as
any watchdog . . . the gun will keep quiet.
. . . It will only open fire if they rush us
. . . but for all it's worth then. . . . Biegler's
on ration fatigue. . . . Where the devil is the
pillbox infant? "

"Here, sir."

The tired face of the volunteer appeared between Scharf and Nuetzel. The spectacled
faery eyes blinked for want of sleep.

"Man alive, it's three o'clock. . . . Get a move on and mind that you get at least one mess tin of food through. . . . If it should turn out to be two you may call me nunky. But if you bring the lot you are certain of a mention in army orders. . . . Carry on. . . . Buzz off, Professor."

Biegler did not buzz but he set off, carrying all the mess tins and freighted with a stack of good wishes for luck. . . .

Ration fatigue! . . .

Only a tiny cog in the huge engine of war, but put it out of action, and the whole machine comes to a standstill. A duty distinguished more for trench mud than for heroic repute, unarmed endurance, and yet at a higher price than any assault on any position!

After the volunteer's departure, Schmalz rehearsed the plan of operations.

"The show must not last longer than two hours. . . . After the thunderstorm we can, it is true, count on thick morning mist. . . . But Lord knows how far Lieutenant Goebel is from the line. . . . I mean the other chap's line. . . . Well, carry on."

The lance-corporal knotted a string of ground sheets and buckled two broad webbing belts round his own body. Before that, he had tested the trustworthiness of the rope.

The crater-field, water-logged and slippery as a sponge after the rain, perforated into innumerable puddles and ruts, was lying a dirty grey under the dark sky. The soil was a ferment and reek of rancid grease.

Private Schramm of the scattered patrol must have had a well-developed bump of locality. At first he covered some fifty yards at the double, then serpentined over a shallow dip, sprinted on again, and plunged into a fairly deep shell hole, the southward face of which he climbed on hands and knees. Keeping the Red Cross man, who adroitly fell in with his every movement, in tow, Schramm now panted in a whisper to him:

" We're all right. . . . The wire is twenty yards ahead of us."

They flattened themselves close against the ground and got their wind back.

When their lungs were breathing more quietly, Hiesinger made the rope clear.

"Look here, matey. . . . I am tying this line round my arm. . . . You'll hold on to the other end. . . . Hope the rope's long enough. . . . If not, it doesn't matter a hoot

62

either. . . . When I give one jerk it means :
I am within sight of the officer. . . . Two
mean : I am up to the officer. . . . Three :
I have picked him up and am coming back.
. . . Catch on? . . . You might jerk occasionally. . . . Then I shall know I'm on
the right track. . . ."

Schramm growled in acquiescence.

" Agreed, pal. . . . I would sooner have
gone out myself. . . . But perhaps I might
catch hold of him wrong. . . . You know
more about that than a chap like me. . . .
And my best respects for the way you can
sprint and stomach crawl. . . . You're an old
hand at the game even if you have a hell of a
lot of back chat. . . . Now you look here.
. . . Follow your nose up the slope . . . then
squirm on ten times your own length, always
following your nose. . . . Mind you keep
direction. . . ."

The bombardment had become more me-
thodical : it had ceased to be spasmodic and
gusty. The front lines were growling at one
another like dogs in the night.

Hiesinger had crawled up the rim of
the shell hole. He saw a tangle of stakes
and wire, indistinct and vague, ahead of

him, a closely tangled, quickset hedge—the wire.

In front of, amid, and behind the wire, little spurts of the bursts were dancing. They were all small calibre stuff.

"Have you got hold of the line, Schramm? I'm pushing off."

On knees and elbows, the Red Cross man worked his way on. He was out of the crater astonishingly quickly. No Red Indian could have done it more skilfully or more noiselessly.

Schramm cowered against the lip of the shell hole, all his senses tense and more than alert.

Then the first jerk came and coursed like an electric shock through Schramm's body. He jerked back to signal that he had understood and again the answer came. Jerk . . . jerk. . . . So he had reached the lieutenant.

The Red Cross man had crawled about ten times his own length, when his ear caught a low moan.

With his ear pressed close against the ground he listened with bated breath. Again the low moan of pain which, unreal and elusive, seemed to emanate from the lips of the earth itself.

64

Slowly Hiesinger raised his head and turned it towards the direction of the sound. In a tiny fold of the ground not more than three paces to his right, he saw two bodies.

The Red Cross man was there in a twinkling.

One body lay dumb and stiff, a puppet whose limbs had been twisted all awry. The other body showed a leg drawn up and cramped against the trunk.

Hiesinger bent over the wounded man. He recognised the officer by the cut of his tunic.

Lieutenant Goebel kept his eyes half closed and stifled a groan between his teeth. He was conscious.

"Steady, mate. . . . Don't let the blighters in front spot us. . . . Where's the trouble?"

"Bullet through the right thigh," the lieutenant replied in a whisper.

"Just take it easy, mate, I am going to take you back. . . . Have only got to throw an eye over the other one first."

With an expert touch the Medical lance-corporal had possessed himself of the dead man's identity disc, and took all the odds and ends he found in the pockets as well.

"Well . . . that's that. . . . And just turn

E   65

a little over on your side. . . . Easy, take it easy. . . . We've got plenty of time."

Skilfully, Hiesinger raised the wounded man on his back, slipped a belt round the lieutenant's armpits and crawled back with his living load. But first he gave three tugs at the line.

Private Schramm would fain have cheered when he got the signal. But he suppressed the inclination and instead, gave relief to his feelings by the careful fashion with which he drew in the rope. The coil of stuff in his hands grew and before long he saw the strange apparition with the double back. Schramm raised his hands over the crater rim, grabbed Hiesinger's shoulders and helped the Red Cross man into the shell hole.

Hiesinger was streaming from every pore.

" He isn't at all heavy. . . . Should say nine stone at most . . . and yet it was the devil's own job. . . . How about a tot, old man? "

The lance-corporal first heaved a sigh and then took a pull at a brand of the right stuff. The water bottle passed on to Schramm.

" What's the matter with the lieutenant? . . . Oh, I see. . . . Fainted! . . . I thought he might have because he kept so extraordinarily quiet all the way here. . . . Doesn't matter a bit. . . . On the contrary. . . . It makes it all the easier."

A light rain set in, really more of a Scotch mist. Far away towards the East, a milky glimmer as narrow as an eye slit. Morning was knocking at the gates of heaven.

"Now let's get a move on. . . . Things are becoming sticky. . . . If we aren't in our flea chest within the next quarter of an hour, we may have to while away the whole day in some shell hole or other. . . . The corporal's lurking in some damned crater behind us. . . . Let's steer for that. . . . I'll pick up the officer and then quick march and no falling out. . . ."

Corporal Schmalz was sitting in his crater, sucking at a cold pipe. He was drowsing half awake, and practising the art, very essential in a soldier's case, of snatching a few winks of sleep in any situation in life or position of body.

He was now roused from his praiseworthy practice. What was the meaning of the sound of footfalls? Who was approaching at the double?

Before the N.C.O. had solved the question, two shadows detached themselves from the darkness and plunged into the crater.

For the space of three minutes he heard nothing round him beyond toilsome intake of breath and spasmodic panting. Then Hiesinger got his vocal apparatus into working order again and gave it free play.

"That you, Corporal? . . . We've got the field marshal all right. . . . I tell you, it was some sprint. . . I tell you, if I did not cover those forty yards—with the officer on my back and in pitch darkness—in faster time than a racing greyhound, I'll eat my lance's buttons. . . . Wasn't much time to waste either. . . . The blighters over there are sitting up and taking notice."

Flashes of rifle fire were flickering in the wire entanglement. The searching fire of a machine-gun buzzed overhead.

Schramm rubbed his shapeless grey hands and chuckled gleefully.

"Thanks very much, Mrs. Meier . . . we've fairly slipped through your fingers. Here's to you, Schnaps. . . . Long life and a merry one."

Hiesinger nodded benevolently, and wiped

the perspiration from his forehead with his coat sleeve.

"Chap must have luck . . . Chap who hasn't any luck in war had better hang himself straight away . . . and there they are blazing all round the landscape and shooting holes in the air. . . ."

The firing was, in fact, reassuringly high and ragged.

Bending over the lieutenant, who was still unconscious, the corporal twisted his jungle of a beard through his fingers meditatively.

"Don't like the look of him. . . Get on, boys, else it will get too light."

The sallow streak in the East had broadened. The night was flaking away like lint being plucked. Without further incident they brought the lieutenant into the pillbox.

There they found Nuetzel beside a second casualty of the patrol.

"That chap was in the shell hole as I passed. . . . Have lugged him in. . . . Poor chap's got a bullet wound below the belt. . . . Sh-Sh. . . . Don't let him see you know."

The wounded man was a broad, heavy fellow, half a head taller than Nuetzel who himself did not look undersized. To drag such a

69

weight over shell holes and hollows had undoubtedly meant more than sweat.

The wounded man's eyes were big and wide open; they passed quietly from face to face. The man did not seem to be in pain for he lay stretched motionless on the plank bed. Lieutenant Goebel was laid beside him.

Hiesinger was all medical service. This usually rough and boisterous male animal outdid any woman for composure of manner and gentleness of movement. He examined the lieutenant's wound, bandaged it, and gave voice to his professional opinion.

" Machine-gun bullet in the right hip . . . slanting shot . . . wound of entry higher than that of exit . . . artery uninjured . . . chap must have luck. . . . Possibly the hip bone's been damaged . . . the loss of consciousness don't signify . . . we'll get him round all right."

Hiesinger blew a big cloud of smoke from his cigarette and turned to the other wounded man.

" Well, mate, let's have a look at you. . . . Looks quite O.K. . . . No, don't move. . . . Nothing to eat or drink for the present. . . . With that shot wound you'll live to be seventy."

The eyes of the wounded man, clear and knowledgeable, followed Hiesinger. His lips moved without uttering a sound. Nuetzel looked at the corporal with meaning. They turned away from the bunk to the gun emplacement. The Red Cross man followed them.

"He'll not live through to-morrow night. . . . Seems to know it himself. . . . Chap must have luck. . . . At any rate he's not in pain. . . . What's about the time, Corporal?"

The hands pointed to exactly four o'clock in the morning.

"Who'd have thought it?" The Red Cross man was astonished. "So the whole show is supposed to have lasted only forty minutes? Those forty minutes might have turned another chap's hair grey."

The rescue of the wounded lieutenant had taken forty minutes.

Hiesinger shook his head incredulously. It had seemed as many hours to him.

¶ Idyll Round the Cooker—The Lentil Santa Claus.

THEY were drumming from every muzzle. A curtain of steel was suspended from horizon to horizon. The wall of grey smoke, splashed with red and yellow in the flashes of the shell bursts, moved restlessly backwards and forwards over a strip of ground of about a hundred yards in depth.

The vault of the firmament broadcasted the roll of the drum fire monotonously. Every other sound was swallowed up in this roll. Except for the level splashing of rain that had set in again since daybreak. This spatter with its distinctive note, held its own obstinately.

Kurt Biegler, the pillbox infant, was standing in the queue of ration orderlies, coiled round the steaming field kitchen.

The cooker had been brought up into the disconsolate wreckage of a barn. Of its erstwhile four walls only two and a half were left. A few charred beams indicated the roof that had disappeared. The rain hissed into the barn without let or hindrance, and formed dull puddles on its uneven floor.

Wrapped up in his ground sheet, the cook orderly stirred an imposing ladle in the cooker and looked glum because the rain was falling into the body of the stew and raising little blisters on its surface.

"We've got water enough of our own. . . . Might rain dripping by way of a change. . . . Don't shove, boys. . . . Every man in his turn."

The cook pushed his greasy service cap out of his eyes and filled the mess tins held out to him, scrupulously careful to see that every man had his fair share of fat and lean. All the time, Fuerstner, the cook, went on grunting and grousing behind his thick, black walrus moustache.

"Ought to give notice by rights. . . . Won't stay another hour in this kitchen. . . . Out at three a.m. in this beastly weather . . . sweating water at four, blood at five . . . told to cook and haven't got any stuff. . . . I'm fed up with the whole bloody war."

This confession of faith was delivered dolefully enough but only roused full-throated mirth. A lanky orderly guffawed whole-heartedly and amid general acclamation gave his views.

"Of course he's got to shove his oar in . . . though he prefers the back area. . . . Sweating blood, is he? . . . What are we sweating in the line? . . . If you don't feel comfy over your stew pots, why don't you send in your name for M.G.'s. . . . There you are! There are my five tins, hike 'em up to the line. . . . I'll carry on and chance it with your ladle."

The proposed exchange did not, however, appear to appeal to Fuerstner in the least. He plunged the ladle into the cauldron and stood with arms akimbo:

"That blinking length of misery can't keep his mouth shut. . . . If he tumbles down, he'll fall into the adjoining sector. . . . You and cooking! . . . That'ud be worth watching. . . .We're lines of communication? . . . You keep your mouth shut. I'm a front line man, almost as dirty as you. . . . Just look at that cooker. . . . See anything?"

Twenty pairs of eyes turned on the cauldron. It was, if not thirty years old, a bit of furniture with a past. The attention it created flattered the cook.

74

"Well! do you see anything? . . . No! Of course you don't. . . . But last week on . . . it's Friday to-day, ten days back . . . on Tuesday my relief—name of Heidner— was on this spot . . . cheery chap. . . . Early morning same as now. . . . Well, he's all right spilling his rotten jokes. . . . All of a sudden there's a smash behind him, over there where only half a wall is left upright. . . . Before the others had time to pull themselves together it was all over. . . . Heidner had fallen over without a squeak. . . . And where was his head? . . . Bobbing about in the middle of that cooker it was. . . . And that long beanstalk yaps about lines of communication. . . . That put the lid on ration issue for that day. . . . Every man got his whack? . . . I am going to get shaved. . . ."

The story of the head in the cooker was confirmed from several quarters. Whereupon an animated debate whether the cooks should be regarded as lines of communication or fighting line ensued. The majority of votes were for the latter.

Beside the cooker against the undamaged wall, the cook was shaved.

A short, undersized stretcher bearer officiated at the ritual and observed all its pre-scribed ceremonial conscientiously.

A time-retired mug served the purposes of a shaving dish, the field kitchen supplied the hot water, and the strap of a saddle-bag a strop for a razor that had qualified for a place in a museum of antiquities.

The cook sprawled luxuriously on the bench, with his legs wide apart, wearing in the top buttonhole of his tunic a blue-checked dish-cloth which appeared to be as badly in need of a shave as the cook himself, so coarse it was to the touch.

The ration orderlies stood about in little groups, smoking and gossiping, to watch the entertainment. Many felt their chins to make sure of their hirsute growth. Most of them had more bristles on their face than the stretcher bearer's shaving brush.*

The man worked away with his shaving brush in the water for all he was worth. He was holding in his hand something, the length of his thumb, that might easily have passed

---

* When we refer to hirsuteness and beards there is no occasion to conjure up visions of full blown foot warmers. The gas mask alone discouraged a full beard. The word " beard " connotes nothing more than a state of the most hideous unshavenness..—Author's Note.

muster for a stick of green cheese. But it was soap, or at any rate purported to be soap.

In any case, this much became clear: the man was trying to get a lather. It was not for want of trying that only a composition that looked very like a watered-down paste and smelt of very inferior tallow was the result. The stretcher bearer plastered both cheeks of the cook with this paste. The brew dissolved into long threads that stuck to the hair like glue.

The stropping of the razor was a side show of its own.

With his left foot on the strap and holding the other end in his left hand, the little beauty artist sawed up and down and accompanied every stroke with a sigh. At length all things appeared to be in readiness. But in the meantime the paste had dried and had to be applied afresh.

Shaving is a test of the nerves, whether a man shaves himself or gets shaved.

Cook Fuerstner was on the far side of all nerves. Not a muscle of his almost circular face, soon bleeding from half a dozen gashes, twitched.

On completion of the ordeal, the cook got

up and stroked his face from ear to ear with the air of a connoisseur.

" It's improving by degrees, little man. . . . Only ten cuts . . . that's fifty per cent better. . . . When you shaved me for the first time it looked like pig sticking. . . . In that case I'd prefer to be scalded like a pig and have my bristles removed with the scraper. . . . It was quite nice to-day. When you're shaved you feel like a human being again."

The " feeling like a human being again " was a daring statement and gave the orderlies occasion for unconcealed amusement. Not a man showed any inclination to submit himself to the knife, although many a beard was itching intolerably.

The little stretcher bearer waved his instrument of torture, that would have graced a chamber of horrors, invitingly, and the cook spoke words of exhortation.

"You all look something chronic . . . all except Biegler . . . and I'd have a beard down to my knees before he had a hair on his face. . . ."

Biegler raised the steel ear-loops of his regulation spectacles and rubbed his rain splashed glasses. He smiled his own quiet smile.

One or two of the group wavered in their determination, but only one of them took his courage in both hands and his seat on the shaving bench.

The tall ration orderly picked up the mess tins.

"I'm off now. . . . Can't stand the sight of blood."

He strode towards the entrance of the barn, but turned again because the cook shouted after him: "Then what are you in the Army for? But as I've always said: the drafts get worse and worse."

Pat and ready came the tall man's retort:

"Same thing with the rations . . . they used to be a lot better."

Before the cook could think of an appropriate repartee, the tall man had passed out, chuckling, into the rain.

It was a signal for departure for the rest of the ration party. Many of them had as much as three hours walk back to the line, not by reason of the distance, but of the obstructions in the way.

In the meantime, the man of valour had been scraped after some blood-letting, and joined them.

Once outside the barn their ways divided.
The groups melted apart. They dispersed
amid rough, but always well meant, parting
shots.

Biegler fell in with a ration orderly of the
forward artillery position. They had a bit of
the way in company. They trudged one behind the other under the grey, cheerless rain
clouds, at first over open country, then through
lines that had been evacuated more than a year
before, to dive into a communication trench on
the other side. Biegler's companion raised his
face to the rain and growled his satisfaction.

"Luck's with us—in this downpour they'll
stay at home with their buses. . . . Nothing
more loathsome than those flying men. . . .
If we don't butt into a barrage and if neither
of us gets drowned in a shell hole, we shall get
the grub home without leaving half of it behind in the mud."

Biegler had a vision of the hunted Nuetzel.
It gave quite a pleasant aspect to the weather.
. . . One was always wet in war whether it
was raining or whether the sun was shining.
The six mess tins of themselves were hot
enough to keep a man perspiring freely.

They rope-danced along the duck boards,

flooring the sole of the trench. The boards were slippery with rain and there were gaps several yards in length. But the duck boards were none the less safer going. A step off them meant that one's boot was plunged up to the knee in the very sticky, adhesive mud. It then became a toss-up whether one succeeded in withdrawing one's boot again or whether it treacherously left its owner in the lurch.

After half an hour's progress, the two ration carriers had a rest. The main communication trench at this point split into three, the central and principal of which led straight into the advanced artillery line. The two subsidiary gullies led, one to the right, the other half left, into the crater-field.

Biegler propped himself beside his companion against the parados and supported himself against the opposite firing step.

" Just lend a hand by holding your overcoat out. . . . I want to light a fag."

In great accord they moved closer and spread out their overcoats against wind and weather. Their united efforts succeeded in getting a cigarette going.

The other blew a cloud of smoke through his nostrils gratefully.

F

"Fags and schnaps . . . but for them I should have thrown my hand in long ago. . . . What puzzles me is how am I going to knock them off later on. . . . Sometime or other there must be peace again. . . . What do you think, matey?"

Biegler thought, as everyone else thought, that the war would be over before winter set in.

The gunner—it was not till then that Biegler discovered his companion's arm of the service from the badges on his collar—spat at his boots and pulled a face registering doubt.

"That's a latrine yarn, matey. . . . I've been in this show from the start and know my way about. The first autumn they told us: 'Before the leaves are off the trees you'll be home.' . . . Tot it up on your fingers how often the leaves have been off the trees since then. . . . The brass hats on top will never stop so long as there's a man left standing upright. . . . Well, for all I care. . . . I didn't start the war. . . . The people who did had damned well better stop it. . . ."

How was Biegler to counter this reasoned argument? He preferred to keep silence and only nodded in his persistently conciliatory way.

The cigarette had been smoked to a finish. The gunner too, seemed to have talked himself out. He got to his feet cumbrously and turned up his dislocated coat collar.

"Well, here's luck, mate. . . . I'm going straight on. . . . Look after yourself."

For a few minutes Biegler looked after the gunner. His shoulders were one moment above, the next, below the ground level, and his figure rocked like a boat left to look after herself in rough water. Then it disappeared in the trench.

The subsidiary cutting half left, which Biegler had to follow was notorious. Only sparingly furnished with duck boards, more than one man had been bogged there up to his middle at the worst places and was lucky to extricate himself by sacrificing a boot or the whole of his foot gear.

Biegler pushed on very cautiously over a succession of pools by testing every single foothold. He knew; a single misjudged step and he'd be having a bath with his six mess tins in one of these brown ponds.

It was strenuous work for a man of poor,

undeveloped physique. The six full mess tins weighed Biegler down like so many lumps of lead, and he was soaked to the skin. His overcoat was saturated, was stiff with mud and its skirts were as unyielding as galvanized iron. Every step meant a struggle with the garment.

With his head burning and wholly played out, Biegler rested in a comparatively dry bit of trench. He supported his arms on his knees and his head rested, worn out, on his hands.

Two years. . . . Short scenes, torn from their context, passed in review. . . .

Kurt Biegler, prize pupil of an art course, had volunteered for service; rejected twice, he had been accepted as fit on a third inspection . . . hadn't he the stale smell of the barracks during his term of training in his nostrils still? . . . He had joined up in the most glorious spring-tide weather. By the time he was drafted to the war zone, the corn was lying in swathes in the fields. For more than a year he had been on duty in the line, quite long enough to adjust romantic imaginings of war by its rough reality. What had this year meant? . . . An alteration of noise and little

84

rest, of hunger, thirst, and dirt and dodging past death that is close to every man in the line and never leaves his elbow. . . . Had not a certain Kurt Biegler visualized quite other pictures of it all? . . . Where was the heady glow of exultation that had swept him, like others, off his feet. . . . Drowned in blood and mud . . . the routine of duty brought out true greatness. . . . Sticking it for days in lousy dug-outs . . . digging in at any hour in any weather . . . the dumb resigned crouching under the tattoo of drum fire . . . the whole monotonous, monosyllabic, uncomplaining serfdom of war.

Hard furrowed faces, eyes, into which all the horror of the times had filtered, flitted through Biegler's brain . . . he felt the grip of horny hands and with their pressure this certainty : one man would be hopelessly lost in this hell . . . this war could be endured only by virtue of this reciprocal support and cheer, by this matter of course self-sacrifice of one man for his fellows.

The realization of it swept hot through Kurt Biegler; the Corporal and Scharf and Nuetzel and the Red Cross man; that was the little world to which Kurt Biegler, budding artist and volunteer M.G. gunner, was linked for better or for worse . . . comradeship . . . comradeship-in-arms.

A shellburst scattered his meditations. Biegler was startled out of his fit of brooding and swiftly thrown back into the needs of the hour.

Not for a second had the drum fire slackened. The right sector was under conspicuously hot fire. His companion of the advanced artillery lines would be in the thick of it.

Every now and then, little yellowish-green clouds formed against the grey wall of smoke, floated out of the reek and sank reluctantly towards the ground. That meant they were sending over gas shells. The rain weighed the heavy cloudlets down. Biegler tested the direction of the wind. The breeze was setting lightly from the West; the danger was therefore not great, but caution was indicated. There was no accounting for the movements of gas. It was easy to get a whiff before there was time to pull a gas mask out of its case.

Wearing a gas mask was not unalloyed delight. It was difficult to breathe at all freely and the rain blurred the goggles so that every-

86

thing was seen through a haze, and in quite a short time the temperature under the snout-like funnel was that of a crucible.

For a moment it was only a toss-up whether Biegler with his six mess tins was in for a ducking or not. His left leg was in the ooze up to the hip and it was only thanks to the chance that his foot happened to strike firmer ground that everything passed off without disaster.

So it was an artist, reduced to his lowest common denominator, that at length reached the angle in the communication trench whence he was within sixty yards of the pillbox. Private Scharf was lurking in the kink, smoking for all he was worth.

"Hurray. . . . the pillbox infant's back. Man alive. . . . The eyes of all wait upon you. . . . And the grub? . . . All six tins. . . . You're worth your place in the family circle, Biegler. . . . You're safe for the putty medal. . . . Hand us the buckets."

Scharf possessed himself of the tins in a twinkling. Biegler took off his gas mask and gasped for air. Beads of perspiration were streaming from his forehead, but behind his exhaustion beamed his quiet, grateful smile.

" Snort away, Professor. . . . Five minutes or so don't matter. . . ."

Scharf raised the lid of a mess tin, inspected its contents suspiciously and sniffed them to make sure. The investigation seemed to afford him satisfaction and evoked a complacent, beaming grin.

Biegler's reception in the pillbox was animated. Schmalz and Nuetzel shook him by the hand half a dozen times over.

" Well done, Biegler. To get back with all the mess tins and not even to have had a roll in the mud is not a bad performance even for an old hand. . . ."

Schmalz's voice had a hearty ring.

From the background, where the Red Cross man was busy with the abdominal case, fluted Hiesinger's voice :

" Congratulations and felicitations, Professor. . . . What's the grub like? "

Scharf waved a tin and chanted as if he were leading the Hallelujah chorus in a village choir :

" Just guess, Schnaps."

The lance-corporal came up, sniffed at the tin and assumed the furrowed brow of a thinker.

"Barbed wire?"

Scharf shook his head at this accepted reference to dessicated vegetables.

"Pease pudding?"

"Wrong again, Hiesinger."

Scharf refrained from keeping the other on the rack any longer.

"Lentils, man . . . just think, lentils, and quite thick. . . ."

If ever a beatific glow can illumine human countenance, it was the expression of Hiesinger's face.

"Lentils. . . . He has brought back lentils. . . . So Biegler's a blinking Santa Claus?"

The reposeful sound of busy mouths and jaws was broken by a groan. The abdominal case was watching the party with hungry eyes.

¶ The Pillbox Shows its Teeth.
¶ One Man Passes Over.

TOWARDS mid-day the fury of the bombardment became doubly furious. Bursts danced all round the pillbox. Its dimly lit interior swayed in an earthquake.

Corporal Schmalz had stationed himself in the gun emplacement and kept a sharp look-through his Zeiss glasses.

The attack on the adjoining sector had developed by this time. Behind the creeping barrage the flat steel helmets of the assaulting troops were visible. The column in long line of single file advanced simultaneously into the crater-field.

Before and between the columns crawled the tanks. Cumbrous yet mobile, the iron caterpillars ate their way into the terrain, crushing everything in their path into the earth and clearing the way for the storm troops. A whole pack of tanks were pushing along a farmhouse road hardly recognizable for what it was.

"One—two—three—four—five," counted the N.C.O., and focused his glasses more steadily on the pack.

The tanks climbed through shell holes and over inequalities of the ground, rose at times in the bow, at times in the stern, like tramp steamers in a heavy sea and spat fire from every slit.

Suddenly the leading tank shot out a jet of flame and burst into a blaze. A second reared like a jibbing horse, jerked backwards once again, and half turned turtle. The others reversed and made off to the rear.

In one sector of the crater line there was some hot hand-to-hand fighting. First flat, then domed steel helmets appeared, intertangled, and then sank into the earth.

Round one particular crater the fighting must have been particularly hot. It lay some eight hundred yards perhaps to the right in a rise of the ground and, though hardly perceptibly, commanded the rest of the terrain. But in that flat plateau fifteen feet stood for hillock, and seventy-five for a hill.

From three sides the attack raged round the crater and cut it off crescent wise. The garrison held on desperately and repulsed attack after attack. When the curtain of steel, smoke, and rain lifted the N.C.O. could even make out incidents of the fighting.

To judge from the stubbornness of its resistance the crater was sheltering the remnant of a M.G. nest. Its guns were combing their field of fire in three directions and, ever and again, pinned the attack to the ground.

A cement strong point, hidden away somewhere or other, proved more effective than even this barrage in checking the attack. This pillbox enfiladed the attack in flank and rear unmercifully and lashed the assault back.

The corporal fairly stared the eyes out of his head but could not discover the site of the strong point, so successfully was the pillbox camouflaged into the terrain.

On the other side, where they must be having a horrible experience of its effectiveness, the artillery searched the ground for the obstructive block, and ploughed up its assumed site with every gun.

But immediately afterwards as soon as the storm troops rose to renew the attack the blast of death again began to blow with icy breath from the self-same spot.

Just as a magnet draws iron filings so did

this hellish shell hole attract the forces of either side on itself. Through the barrage, their own as well as the enemy's, the supporting troops filtered into its zone and were forthwith swallowed up in the welter.

Death, insensate, continued to dance on the same spot for hours, for days together. . . .

The corporal knew the scene by heart. It was no new experience. He directed his glasses on the ground immediately in front and to the left of the pillbox but could see no signs of movement and shouted into the interior :

" Things look pretty lousy on the right . . . Scharf, relieve me for half an hour. . . ."

The order was after Scharf's own heart. Observation was his special sport as athletics or swimming might be that of other people.

Schmalz gave him some instructions on the general situation and changed places with his relief.

Lieutenant Goebel had recovered consciousness some two hours previously and his brain was quite clear. He was lying, supporting his head in his right hand, on the plank bed and was listening, for the sixth time, to the Red Cross man's report of how he had been brought in. He had also had some lentils because

Hiesinger simply insisted on it on the ground that a " foot case "—Hiesinger laid special emphasis on the word "foot"—was bound to take nourishment wherever and however he could find food. Apart from that the lieutenant had been honestly hungry. No further reason for eating lentils need be adduced.

The lieutenant, a slightly built man in his early thirties, was not an imposing figure. Only the clever, kindly eyes invested his face with a charm that made its frigid, beardless insignificance attractive. His face at the moment had a look of pain suppressed by force of will. The eyes were uneasy and shone restlessly.

Hiesinger, always of a matter-of-fact disposition, recognized the symptoms of pyrexia and made no secret of his diagnosis.

"May have a touch of fever, Sir. . . . It need not necessarily be so, but it may be. . . . In such cases preventive measures are indicated. . . . In my own case I drink schnaps, a lot of schnaps, and if it doesn't have the desired effect—at once—more schnaps. If it does a man good it doesn't do him any harm . . . only it isn't everyone who can stand it. But then there's another medicament. . . ."

He was rummaging for the other medicament in his medical pannier. It was the inevitable aspirin, Fritz's universal panacea, to which he always had recourse, whether he were suffering from enteritis or from any wound anywhere between the top of his spinal column and his toes.

Lieutenant Goebel smiled. Whether the other medicament or the zeal of the representative of the Army Medical Service, who had become altogether immersed in his professional avocations, amused him is an open question. But he swallowed the two aspirin tablets obediently.

Corporal Schmalz made his report on the position of and the instructions to strong point 17 to the officer. He delivered it in concise soldierly style. The lieutenant listened very attentively, asked a few questions of detail, and was before long very favourably impressed by the efficient and clearheaded personality of the N.C.O. in charge. Schmalz stood to attention in smart, but not atrophied bearing in front of the plank bed and had a clear, intelligent answer for every question put to him.

Lieutenant Goebel had the gift of finding

the right note in his dealings with other ranks. Concise and definite as were the instructions he gave, his tone was neither overbearing nor too superior.

He shook hands warmly with Private Schramm, who had fallen in beside the corporal, and expressed his pleasure at the officer's rescue in uncouth, hearty words. The handshake conveyed as, between men, all the recognition needful and did honour to private and lieutenant alike.

A dull thud made the pillbox stagger. Nuetzel, dozing on an ammunition box, fell from his couch and was sitting in wide eyed astonishment on the floor before he knew where he was.

Scharf called out from the gun emplacement:

"Nothing to worry about . . . a twelve or fifteen-pounder has dropped on the roof . . . and that'll stand up to quite different sort of stuff. . . ."

As no second impact followed it probably was a case of chance, not an aimed, shot.

In spite of that the N.C.O. climbed on the lance's shoulders and examined the ceiling. There was no trace of any damage done.

96

" If there's nothing to be seen from the out-side, we've got away with it again. . . . For chipped cement shows up white and is visible at a considerable distance and doesn't offer a bad mark."

This matter-of-fact explanation from the corporal stirred mixed emotions. Nuetzel and Schramm volunteered at once to investigate, but Schmalz would not have it.

" Investigate what? . . . For the chaps over there to see you and take steps accordingly. . . . Are you trying to make sure of giving our funk hole away? . . . And you needn't take that showing up white too literally. . . . Since when does anything show up white if it's raining? . . . And before the sun's out again they'll have chucked enough mud on the roof to prevent anything from having much chance of showing up. . . . No, stay where you are, lads. . . . We're quite comfy here."

Hiesinger, who could not help picking up every conversational thread and drawing it out, did not miss this chance. The Red Cross man had undoubtedly, immediately on birth, apos-trophized a startled world in a disquisition. He removed the everlasting cigarette from his mouth and twiddled it between his thumb and first finger—

"Well, the corporal is right enough once again. . . . At Fertun we were sprayed in a dug-out for thirty hours in accordance with all the rules of the game. And why? . . . simply because some silly ass couldn't keep his fat head under cover. . . ."

Hiesinger would have enjoyed elaborating the matter of the fat head. But his flow of eloquence was checked by the moaning of the abdominal casualty.

The man was still lying in the posture in which the Red Cross man had placed him. He was a huge fellow, of athletic build, and so tall that his legs outstretched the bunk half-way up his calves. His face looked spongy and revealed greenish-grey patches above the cheek bones, sure symptoms of a decay there was no arresting. Between those spongy patches were deep sunk eyes of a colour hard to determine, eyes that withdrew from the light, hesitant and slowly, like pools doomed to drain out.

But it was not the pain of his wound that made the man moan deeply:

"Thirst, orderly, thirst. . . . Give me

something to drink . . . or I shall fetch it for myself. . . ."

Hiesinger knew what he was up against: the man was now asking for certain death. To eat or drink with a wound of that nature simply meant the surrender of life.

A man's nerves cease to flutter where life and death are concerned after some three dozen lives have slipped through his fingers.

Quick as a flash and yet with great deliberation, Hiesinger thought it out: How long could the man hold on? A few hours at most. . . . There was no fever. . . . So the body had already quite given up resisting. . . . Get him back. . . . No chance of it before the nightfall and then for a dead certainty quite superfluous. . . . So why should not the man have his drink? Everyone in the long run has his last wish that may not be denied him.

The Red Cross man was at peace with his own conscience. He took the wounded man's hand:

"You want a drink? . . . Only don't reproach me for it afterwards. . . . You know what you're about? . . ."

The wounded man nodded unmoved, keeping his gaze steadily fastened on the other.

Hiesinger returned the gaze just as steadily and unmoved.

"Right, pal. . . . You shall have your drink. Neat schnaps or neat water? . . . You'll have a proper mixture of schnaps and water, if you follow my advice."

The wounded man only nodded again.

The Army Medical Service orderly brought the mixture prescribed in the lid of a mess tin. It worried neither him nor his patient that fragments of lentils were floating about in it. Who would be as fussy as all that?

The wounded man drank without haste, with deliberate enjoyment and did not allow the tiniest drop of the brew to run to waste. Then he raised his trunk and asked for a cigarette.

Four hands were simultaneously outstretched towards him. Biegler, Nuetzel, the Red Cross man and the lieutenant handed him cigarettes. The N.C.O. was unable to contribute to this compassionate offering. He smoked a pipe only.

The four contributions were by no means too many for the wounded man's acceptance. He took all the cigarettes and piled them up beside him and, selecting a fag with strict

impartiality, lit it against Hiesinger's cigarette.

With a solemnity as if he were aware of the
last gifts life has to dispense, he puffed the
smoke straight in front of him and followed
the little blue clouds with his eyes.

No one spoke a word. An oppressive silence
descended on the gathering, and with this
silence a foretaste of the grave and of dissolu-
tion. The intake and output of breath were,
apart from the lip movements of the smokers,
the only sounds heard against the reverberation
of the din of battle, dull and ominous, like the
roar of far-off cascades.

Who does not know these moments when
all life seems to have ebbed out of us and the
human soul feels like a leaky vessel, doomed to
go under?

Even Hiesinger, who usually talked all
sense of foreboding off his chest, succumbed to
the heaviness of this mood and kept silent. He
peered dolefully in Nuetzel's direction, but
found only a grim expression of awe in the
latter's face and hurried his gaze on to Biegler.

The volunteer's eyes were peering behind
their spectacles like those of a child listening to
an age-old fairy tale. The corporal was hold-

ing his pipe awry in his mouth and was puffing disconsolately.

Then a loud shout tore this atmosphere of reverence to ribands.

Scharf had turned round on the gun emplacement, and waving his hands excitedly in the air, shouted :

"They're coming, they're coming."

Two bounds up the five-spragged ladder to the platform and the N.C.O. was crouching at the observation slit.

Eighty yards in front of the pillbox the column, man behind man in single file, was groping its way forward, passing the pillbox on a half left front.

The hour of duty had struck.

The words of his orders appeared before the corporal's eyes :

"Open fire only on massed targets in front or half left." The voice of the N.C.O. in charge rang out :

"Get all clear . . . Scharf, up here . . . Biegler, ammunition. Nuetzel, to entrance hole with bombs. . . . Gun ready to open fire."

It went like clockwork. In three movements Scharf had the machine-gun ready to open fire and stood astraddle behind the sights. The volunteer hauled the nearest ammunition box on to the emplacement, tore open the lid and took out two belts. The corporal pressed his thumb downwards, a sign that machine-gunner Scharf at once understood.

Tak-tak-tak. . . . Taktak—taktak. . . . Taktaktak.

The irritated stutter of the machine-gun rang maddening echoes through the pillbox.

Like a hailstorm on a ripe cornfield the searching fire swept the column and mowed down man after man. The formation scattered like a broken chain and fell apart in its constituent links.

The counterfire was ragged. It was far too high to do much damage.

Corporal Schmalz lowered his field glasses.

"They're done. . . . Only thing is whether they've spotted us? . . . We shall know in a minute or two. . . . Cease fire, Scharf. . . . We are not potting individual units. . . . And if one of 'em should run his nose against the pillbox. . . ."

Scharf drew the lever over, without changing his posture. He stayed astride, crouched behind the gun.

Outside, a flat steel helmet separated itself from the ground and raised itself by inches till the head and chest of the scout were in view.

Schmalz focused the man in his glasses. He saw a young, terror-stricken face, tanned by wind and weather, and muddied now by the sticky, rain-soaked soil.

The man turned his head cautiously away from the pillbox towards the left. There was heavy firing from that quarter.

Extended in sparse lines, three, four waves, one behind the other, they charged in attack or counter offensive across the crater field. The guns on either side were drumming the devil's tattoo into their ranks. Not three paces away from the pillbox a man crumpled up in full career and fell on his face. Hit in the chest. A little further to the left another flung up his arms and collapsed backwards. Hit in the head.

The assaulting column opposite re-formed. A furious barrage fell between the column and the pillbox and curtained the one from sight of the other. Slowly the creeping barrage thudded past and when it was raging behind the strong point, Schmalz and Scharf saw the assaulting column advancing in close formation, its front facing further to the left than in the first attack.

The flank and rear lay completely bare to the enfilading fire of the machine-gun.

A motion of the hand from the corporal: Scharf pressed down until his thumbs ached and fired belt after belt which Biegler held ready.

Riddled in front, from the left, in the rear, the column broke for the nearest shell holes. Half its strength, dead or wounded, stayed behind.

Scharf was swearing in a low voice. The gun had jammed in its most rapid fire and in his zeal to make good the breakdown, he had run his hand against the red hot jacket. He was therefore swearing and flapping his right hand which on thumb and first finger displayed handsome blisters.

"Old owl!" he scolded himself, "brought up on M.Gs. and still as stupid. . ."

Nuetzel raced up.

"Corporal! . . . They are in our communication trench. . . . At least a platoon with two M.Gs. One gun is dug in at the bend."

That was bad news. How were they to get out of the pillbox when the time came to evacuate it? By what road were rations to be brought up?

The corporal bit his lip.

"That's rotten luck . . . but there's nothing to be done about it at present. . . . Our people are sure to counter attack and will chuck the blighters out. . . . At any rate, let's hope so."

Schmalz had a conference with the lieutenant. The officer, too, was in favour of taking no action for the moment, and of quietly awaiting the course of events. Only the outpost at the pillbox's entry should be pushed a little forward and doubled.

Schramm and Nuetzel fared forth with bombs after the lieutenant had enjoined them urgently to follow every movement in the trench but to keep out of sight themselves and to report every sign of danger to the pillbox at once.

Twice again did the pillbox open fire that afternoon. On each occasion with shattering effect.

But for all that there were glum faces that evening. The communication trench continued to be occupied.

Only one was carefree and quite at peace.

The abdominal case had done with life.

The last cigarette was hanging half-smoked between his fingers.

It must have been a very gentle death for the hand, holding the cigarette had fallen on his breast as a tired leaf falls to the ground in autumn.

Before it went out, the cigarette had burnt a neat round hole in the tunic, close above the dead man's heart.

¶ A Successful Solo—An Unsuccessful Sally.

THERE was no doubt about it, Pillbox 17 was cut off, but it had not been located.

Nuetzel's report had been correct. That same night, Corporal Schmalz, with Biegler and Scharf, reconnoitred the position.

They had crawled up the communication trench to within five yards of the bend, close to the M.G. dug in there.

For one moment the corporal toyed with the daring scheme of blowing up the gun. Three bombs, concentrated into a single charge, would do the trick. But what then? Schmalz gave up the scheme and went on listening to the clink of trenching tools and spades. They were deepening the trench and consolidating it provisionally. On a breadth of twenty yards, so far as it was possible to estimate by night, they had wired themselves in for the time being.

By the end of an hour the scouts had returned to the pillbox.

The rain still persisted.

Lieutenant Goebel had fallen asleep and it must have been a pretty deep sleep, for beside the plank bed, Hiesinger, Nuetzel and Schramm were playing a game of solo whist conducted on lines reminiscent of a third-rate selling plate meeting.

Hiesinger was making most noise. The lance-corporal looked upon himself as a finished strategist at solo whist and consequently on the other players as duds. This time it was Schramm's turn to undergo instruction.

"My dear good idiot. . . . Where did you learn to play solo? . . . Not from me, otherwise I would return your tuition fees on the spot. . . . He goes and leads the ace of a suit of which I, as second hand have the uncovered king. . . . That's an offence against public morals."

There are card players who cannot stand conversation during the game, Nuetzel was one of them.

"Don't make speeches Schnaps. . . . When it comes to your turn they'll have to make a special job of putting a sock in your mouth . . . else you'll be yapping in the trench grave."

Nuetzel was not very far wrong in this comment of his, for that very reason it gave Hiesinger offence.

"Well, I suppose a fellow may put in a word. . . . I agree you only have a mouth for stoking and smoking. . . ."

This challenge of Hiesinger's developed into a wordy warfare. The code of good manners was a little strained in the course of it, but that did not exorcise the spirit of good fellowship.

Schramm, to whose address the rebuke had really been directed, had not turned a hair under Hiesinger's strictures. He only grinned and brought his fist down hard on the top of the box.

"Are you two going to back chat or are we going on with the game? . . . The Red Cross man talks an awful lot if he gets bored. . . . On the other hand I have a couple of ears. . . ."

The game went on amid a lot of blasphemy, the scratching of heads and little attempts at sharp practice.

When the Red Cross man lost a big hand, he made a scene about it. This put his gifts for the part of heavy father beyond all doubt. At first he gazed at the others dumbfounded, then he counted his tricks over three times and fell to shaking his head faster and faster. But the game was and remained lost by five tricks. Whereupon the Lance heaved a sigh starting in the region of his big toe and clasped his hands above his head like a man watching his house being burnt down.

The gesticulation with the hand was a trifle overdone. Hiesinger's hand hit something hard and tried to push it away. It was the boots of a dead man. Stiff and rigid the body lay on the plank bed. A ground sheet covered the face.

The encounter sobered the despairing gambler.

Silent scorn was written there for losses quite other than that of a solo doubled.

Yet none of them thought of stopping. Schramm egged the lance-corporal on.

"Hurry up, Schnaps. . . . The night's getting on. . . . The luck'll change. . . . And your solo wasn't by any means such a dead snip as you thought."

Whether it was that Hiesinger was really rattled or that he was trying to force his luck he suddenly had the most appalling run of bad luck and kept on paying out. Schramm and

Nuetzel made the most of the fun while it lasted and gleefully worked out how they meant to spend their winnings in the canteen. For three and six, so Nuetzel promised himself, you can have a really gaudy evening that'll buck you up again. And the cream of it is that the medicine man'll pay the tally.

Hiesinger's temper did not improve in adversity. It is not given to everyone to lose with propriety. The lance-corporal was not one of them.

"If the devil's carried off the cow, he may as well have the halter. . . . I'll show you. . . ."

Hiesinger only succeeded in showing that it is no good trying to force your luck at cards. He lost and lost whatever he went, and quarrelled in ungentle terms with God and man.

The hullabaloo woke Lieutenant Goebel. He rubbed his eyes and had to make an effort to remember where he really was. Then he consulted his wrist watch which he wore on a broad strap on his right wrist. The faintly luminous hands pointed to 3.35 a.m. According to that he had slept for nearly five hours and he felt all the better and stronger for it, too. A sudden movement, however, made his hip burn like fire and reminded him of his wound.

The corporal reported the course of his reconnaissance.

"We're in a trap, sir—the shell holes on the right and on the left are occupied. . . . That wouldn't be much to worry about. . . . But they've dug themselves into the communication trench, as well . . . fifty yards to the right of the pillbox they've got a machine-gun in position. . . ."

The lieutenant did not like this last item of news at all. The card party, too, who had hitherto continued to play unperturbed, broke off the game and listened. Lieutenant Goebel gnawed his thumb nail.

"That's a damned bore, Corporal. Nothing to be done about it at the moment. . . . I am counting on our counter attack."

As if only waiting for his cue, Volunteer Biegler burst into the atmosphere of tension. He was on outpost duty at the pillbox entrance. Biegler turned to the corporal. He did not see the lieutenant at first:

"Our crowd's attacking. . . . They are at most twenty paces behind the pillbox. . . ."

Heedless of his wound, Lieutenant Goebel

jumped up. His left foot doubled up and he had to hold on to the bunk. A deep line showed from his nostrils to the corners of his mouth.

" Now or never, men. . . . If we mean to get away out of this hole, this very minute may perhaps be our last chance. . . . Corporal, take every man available with you— except one to stand by at the gun. . . . You know; the M.G. emplacement in the trench. . . . It's got to be abolished. . . ."

Schmalz recalled his plan of operations of the previous night. Its execution was now not only possible, but attractive and urgent. He ordered Scharf to the gun and was about to detach Nuetzel in support. The lieutenant, however, nominated himself for the job. He'd have to manage the few steps somehow. Everyone saw that it was only by the exertion of all his strength that Lieutenant Goebel kept on his feet at all.

The N.C.O. made his disposition of his little force. He and Nuetzel would take the lead, Schramm and Biegler would follow close on their heels. Every man equipped himself lavishly with bombs. Nuetzel and the corporal with a concentrated charge apiece as well.

Outside, dawn was breaking in a drizzle, that half and half light between night and day that precedes every sunrise. A fine, wet mist blurred everything and smudged every sharp outline. The German counter attack was developing strongly. Furious artillery and rifle fire was holding it up. From two or three points in the German line rose green rockets, a signal that the German artillery was limping behind the attack and was checking the advance by firing short.

On the line of the pillbox, the attack had come to a complete standstill. The machine-gun in the communication trench! . . . It swept an area of a hundred yards in depth and commanded even the narrowest loophole for infiltration.

Corporal Schmalz had crawled out of the pillbox at the head of his small force and was now almost halfway. At his side, Nuetzel was squeezing himself tight against the other side of the trench. Schramm and Biegler followed in such close attendance that they barked their noses on Schmalz' and Nuetzel's heels.

The machine-gun was grinding away monotonously from the trench. The distance from its emplacement was at most twenty yards. The heads and shoulders of the two men serving the gun were distinctly visible. They had their backs turned and eyes only for what was going on in front of them.

Only for a fraction of a second did the N.C.O. take stock of the position. Everything depended on the suddenness of the surprise. The machine-gun had to be knocked out before there was time to switch it round. A flicker of the eyelids to Nuetzel, a sign with the hand stretched out behind him and without a sound the storm troop dashed for the gun. Five yards before the kink in the trench the corporal hurled the first bomb.

If someone were to tear a half-inch tin plate from top to bottom, he might reproduce a similar screeching noise. Nuetzel's bomb, nicely judged and bursting right up against the machine-gun, followed the corporal's at once. The concentrated charge completed the coup.

The gun was silenced.

Apparitions in field grey emerged close to Nuetzel and the corporal. They had seized their opportunity and dashed breathless for the trench.

Everything was in confusion there. The raid from that quarter was too sudden and unexpected and, above all, from a direction that made resistance pretty well impossible.

With a bound, Nuetzel and the N.C.O. reached the silenced machine-gun. The belt was still hanging half-fired in the gun.

A rapid survey, three or four expert movements and the gun was reversed and spitting straight up the long stretch of trench. There was, of course, no holding it. Every one of its occupants able to fly, fled precipitately. Every man who stayed behind was either dead or wounded.

The storm troop from Pillbox 17 consolidated its position in the trench. Nuetzel flung himself down behind the captured gun, now turned against the enemy, Corporal Schmalz blew his nose with gusto.

"That's that, boys. . . . Didn't take us three minutes. . . . Now it's up to us to exploit the position. . . . Schramm will proceed to the pillbox and report to the lieutenant for ration fatigue. . . . Just take all the feeding tins you can lay your hands on. . . ."

Nuetzel approved strongly of this order. He stimulated Schramm, who was lying beside him, to haste. Haste was in fact indicated for they had recovered from the surprise on the other side.

An unpleasantly accurate retaliation shoot was in progress. From the nearest crater came a very ominous report.

The N.C.O. kept the spot under close observation. With an almost soothing, gurgling sound, a black object screwed itself into the air, wobbled about a few times at the height of its trajectory, as if it were trying to remember something and then hurtled down, swift as an arrow from the height. A deafening roar and a huge crater at the point of impact were the final effects.

"Flying pig," Nuetzel crowed to the corporal. The corporal puckered his brow at the far from pleasant surprise. But there was not much time to spare for furrowed brows or any similar intellectual manifestation.

Every successive discharge from the Minnenwerfer became more troublesome. It was a matter of calculation to within a quarter-of-an-hour when the trench would have to be evacuated under this treacherous bombardment. Treacherous and low down, that was the general opinion of the Minnenwerfer.

One of those tin portmanteaus about the height of a man would wobble, gurgling jovially, up to a certain height. It was not in the least difficult to follow its ascent with the naked eye. But then things became more dangerous to life and limb than they normally are in war. The wobble at the height of the trajectory confounded every sense of direction. The danger of running straight into the burst always had to be taken into account, because the descent occurred with a manifold greater velocity than the ascent.

Every man in the trench knew that, and everyone alike was boiling with wrath at the Minnenwerfer.

But what was to be done about it?

Half-a-dozen bombs would have done the trick. But the range was too great for a trustworthy throwing distance. The German artillery either had failed to spot the disagreeable interloper or was afraid of firing into its own lines.

The situation was becoming critical, more especially as on the other side they were preparing to renew the attack. The Minnenwerfer bombardment crept ever closer to the trench. One shell had already burst in the middle of it. There was no holding that spot any longer.

The pillbox party owed it only to the kink in the communication trench that they were not affected. But they moved a few yards closer to their cement stronghold none the less.

Nuetzel nudged the N.C.O.

"Things are pretty stuffy, Corporal. . . . The blighters over there are up to something. . . ."

By way of answer came a shattering roar that made every man's bones vibrate. Splinters and lumps of earth whizzed past their nose and ears and a wave of wet mud swept over them.

That put the lid on it. A Jack Johnson of a calibre that turns whole trenches into graves, had burst in front of them.

Out of the reek of the explosion figures emerged. They raced up in long strides. The attack sagged away under rifle fire. A spell of quiet ensued. The Minnenwerfer, too, had knocked off work. No one enquired why. The fact was quite enough for the fighting man.

Schramm crawled past behind the pillbox

party. He shouted to Nuetzel and the corporal and waved his mess tins.

"Here's to you, Nuetzel. . . . To you, Corporal . . . to you, volunteer. . . . Carry on with the good work."

The round, amazingly dirty face laughed once more and displayed its splendid teeth. Then Schramm disappeared into the bowels of the trench.

The day had more than dawned. After the rain it held promise of bright sunshine.

The N.C.O. scanned the morning sky anxiously. Nuetzel knew what the scrutiny portended.

"Won't have to wait long, Corporal. . . . Gussie's had to lie low for two days. . . . She's sure to make up for it to-day."

Half-an-hour passed uneventfully except for the customary shelling.

But then, amid the usual din of battle a new note struck the ear, a rattle and rumble, a noisy thudding and throbbing, a panting and creaking that sounded as if it were issuing from a metal megaphone. Between the craters, fifty yards to the right of the communication trench, and the trench itself, a steel monster appeared panting from every vent hole. The tank rolled up in a zigzag course and, swinging round on the trench, opened fire from every slot.

And then the airman appeared on the scene.

He rushed up behind the tank at a height of some thirty feet and swept the trench lengthwise with machine-gun fire.

Scattered units slipped out of the trench and sought cover in the rear. Most of them fled up the trench towards the kink where the pillbox party were lying behind their captured gun.

At this point the fugitives tied themselves in a knot that offered the plane a target it could not miss.

Corporal Schmalz leapt to his feet shouting:

"Follow me, follow me," into the turmoil for all his lungs were worth.

But for many a man the last forty yards to shelter was the last race with death. When the last man had taken cover in the pillbox, the airman circled some ten times round the spot where his quarry had given him the slip so suddenly and mysteriously.

In addition to the members of its original garrison, another four men succeeded in taking refuge in the strong point, two of whom were casualties. One of them was a youngster in khaki, a Canadian.

Pillbox 17, four paces long by three wide, had a garrison eleven strong. It consisted of one dead man and ten other men in purgatory, three of them wounded.

¶ They have spotted It.
¶ Parched Tongues.

THE sun was still climbing to his noontide zenith and his rays were even then falling on the re-occupied communication trench. The way was therefore barred for the second time. Worse still: Pillbox 17 was located.

Three times the aeroplane returned to the spot where the pillbox party had disappeared into the earth. It cruised about low over this spot and pried into every fold of the ground. At length it appeared to have made sure and sped off.

For an hour, artillery and Minnenwerfer fire had raged on the purlieus of the pillbox and maintained a box barrage round the cement block. It was completely isolated.

As good luck would have it there were at first, few direct hits. The water-logged soil sapped high explosive a good deal of its effect.

Further succour came from the German guns. They kept the communication trench and the adjoining crater under murderous fire and nipped every attempt at an advance in the bud.

The shelter was as tightly packed as a barrel of herrings. Nor was its savour much more inviting. Ten men were sharing a space of twelve feet by nine. Every man was smoking and doing his best to empest the atmosphere. The sweetish penetrating scent of opiate in Turkish tobacco that was noticeable above the other smells, came from a cigarette the young Canadian, a well-grown, smart looking young fellow, was smoking. His kit and equipment were of the best. The full round face told of plentiful fare and was in strong contrast to the pinched haggard faces of the pillbox party.

The man in khaki had a bullet wound through both cheeks. As a result of this wound the lower half of his face was swollen and looked like a well developed dumpling. Hiesinger found renewed occasion to marvel at the way of the world. He diagnosed clean penetration without injury to jaws, teeth or tongue, bandaged the Canadian and received a beaming, if only partially successful, smile.

The restless curiosity of the Red Cross man was stirred, but the attempt to establish communications failed. The Canadian knew no

German and Hiesinger no English except six words and all six applied to something to eat, to drink, or to smoke. The Lance had to give utterance to his feelings and because the corporal was at hand he addressed himself to him:

"These Tommies are stout fellows—wonderful performers at the grub stakes. . . . But as tongue-tied as stock fish. . . . That chap came from Canada. . . . If it were possible to exchange a word of sense with one born at seven months, I should ask him. . . . Do you know what I should ask him, Corporal? . . . I should ask him why he travelled five thousand miles or more in a ship—only to have a hole drilled in his face. . . . What damned fools they must be."

The corporal had no opportunity of answering because the lieutenant was beckoning to him.

The lieutenant wanted to examine the Canadian. Corporal Schmalz brought the man up but the lieutenant did not succeed in establishing any means of communication. The brown giant, half a head taller than any of the rest of them, only flapped his ears and pointed to his wound. He offered no objection to the examination of the many pockets, embodied in his tunic in very workmanlike fashion. In fact, he lent a hand.

Tobacco, cigarettes, chocolate, notebook, pencils, first aid dressings, a miniature electric torch and an oblong box containing a grey unguent. These treasures were exhibited in the light of the pillbox. They were all returned to their owner except for the notebook and the torch.

The lieutenant pocketed the torch and glanced through the notebook, but only found addresses and drafts of letters. The man was little more than an innocuous deserter. But he had to be deprived of the torch as the only guarantee against the idea of signalling occurring to him one night.

The next moment the Canadian was distributing cigarettes and tobacco. He did it with a grin which his wound and thick head bandage turned into a cheerful grimace.

The comforts were thoroughly welcome and false pride did not prevent anyone from accepting them.

The corporal loaded his pipe for all it would hold and registered the marked difference between the German issue tobacco and the splendid weed of the man in khaki. Nuetzel, Hiesinger and Scharf squeezed up their eyes and nearly dribbled in ecstasy in the enjoyment of their cigarettes, which enjoyment the Red Cross man endorsed by thoughtful comment.

"The blighters aren't short of anything. . . . That isn't the case with us poor folk. . . . No one under the rank of field officer would smoke fags like these on our side. . . . You haven't to wear a gas mask for stuff like this. . . ."

Epigrams, brain splinters of this sort, the lance-corporal turned out in ample supplies and scattered them lavishly over the pillbox. Brain splinters, however, are not shell splinters, but none the less may find their mark, as often occurred in the case of the Red Cross man's *obiter dicta*. It was a long time since Hiesinger had had such an attentive audience and it stimulated him to talk thirteen to the dozen. His wonderful gift of the gab was winning new admirers.

One of the three Germans who had taken refuge in the pillbox, could hardly take his eyes off the medical orderly's lips. Admiration and impatience were struggling for mastery in his gaze.

Hiesinger had at length to come to a halt. The man with the reverently impatient expression seized his opportunity; and inquired politely whether the lance-corporal had by any chance dined off goose giblets since it all flowed out of him so smoothly, because if his digestion were like his flow of language there was no danger of constipation. The man spoke with an immobile face but in a tone of voice that gave promise of ample resources of acrid commentary.

Now, the Red Cross man was of a combative disposition and not a little vain of his gift of eloquence. He resolved to pluck the tail feathers of the cockerel that dared to crow so impudently. He was on the point of opening his mouth for this purpose. But he got no further. His adversary simply plucked him by the coat sleeve and drew him to the plank bed.

There, sitting on an ammunition box, resting his head against the wooden rim of the bunk, was a little weakly man with such a tiny face that a man's hand might have covered it. The man was whining gently and pressing his hand against his right side.

So far as Hiesinger was concerned, everything was forgotten and forgiven. He bent over the casualty and examined his injuries. Then he turned to his erstwhile critic:

"Man! . . . Why didn't you take me over before? That long blighter from Canada could easily have waited. . . . The chap's got a nasty chest wound."

A shrug of the shoulders was the only response.

When once called upon to succour, the lance-corporal was a changed man, intent only upon real service and, with it all, as laconic as a good housewife at spring-cleaning.

The plank bed was occupied, the lower bunk by the lieutenant whose hip wound prevented him from climbing, the upper one by the dead man, whose stiffly outstretched figure had almost disappeared in clouds of tobacco smoke.

Hiesinger was not at a loss. He called to Scharf and Nuetzel:

"Just help me re-form the chap up there. . . . His place is wanted for the little fellow. . . ."

Lowering the heavy body from the upper bunk involved sweat and hard work. The dead man was accommodated in a scoop of the pillbox with his face against the cement wall. From the hips upwards, he rose above the floor level and sat there half erect like an Egyptian portrait bust in stone.

The transport of the little man with the baby face was, on the other hand, an easy matter. After the Red Cross man had washed and bound up the wound in his chest, he took the little fellow in his arms and lifted him into the upper bunk. Hiesinger manipulated his patient as if he were egg-shell china. The Red Cross man thereby won the honest admiration of his erstwhile critic. The latter voiced his opinion that there was a lot of good stuff in Hiesinger and that, in addition to his jawbone, he had a lot of other things in their right place. If the Red Cross man enjoyed it, he could go on talking till the Day of Judgment because, after all, conversation had to be kept going.

After a job of work, the medical orderly was always inclined to be conversational. But like all people who talk a lot, he was shy of irony in so far as it did not emanate from himself. Nor did the sarcastic style of the other appeal to him.

And finally : talking makes one feel thirsty.

Of the seven plagues of the man in the trenches—hunger, thirst, dirt, rats, cold, wet, and lice—thirst is the worst. To have to starve for three or four days does no one any particular harm, but to have to go without a drink for only half a day, knocks the stuffing out of even the toughest.

The pillbox had the temperature of a laundry ironing room, that dry, parching heat that breeds thirst and yet more thirst.

But every water bottle rang hollow when tapped, and shaking proved of no avail. No heartening gurgle responded.

The only water left was in the water-jacket of the M.G. and some schnaps in the lance-corporal's first-aid flask. But it never occurred to anyone to drink them because both, the water and the schnaps in question, had to be reserved for cases of direst emergency.

Scharf, the gunner on duty and the thirstiest soul in the place, ticked Nuetzel off in style because he ventured on a timid hint at the contents of the water-jacket.

" By all means. . . . Suppose you've gone a bit dotty, Scheps! . . . You drink that water and don't mind if I use my gun for a

132

coffee grinder, but not for shooting. . . .
What do you imagine really? "

Nuetzel did not really imagine anything at
all. It was simply thirst finding utterance and
that imagines one thing only : drink.

"What are you making such a beastly coil
about? . . . I only thought before it evapor-
ates. . . ."

The afternoon crept on in an atmosphere of
deep depression. The men squatted about in
the pillbox dispirited, gasped for air and
smoked desperately in order to keep their
saliva active. That, at least, kept the worst
pangs of thirst under control. They were all
tongue-tied, even the Red Cross man.

The faint hopes that Schramm, the ration
orderly, might yet get through, was abandoned
at last. With an oath that was half a sigh,
Nuetzel killed and buried this hope.

"Schramm won't get through. . . . Not
that I care about the grub. . . . He wouldn't
bring anything else in any case. . . ."

Hiesinger made an effort to respond.

"You are probably right, worse luck, about
Schramm not getting through. . . . Oh,
damn it, the heat. . . . And nothing to
drink. . . . The few drops of schnaps in the

flask are for the wounded. . . . They wouldn't do us any good, at best make the thirst worse. . . ."

For all that, Nuetzel shot a yearning glance at the capacious flask. He smacked his lips at the sight.

" You know me, Schnaps, you know I never was a skrim-shanker. . . . But thirst knocks the guts out of me. . . . Once, it was on the ' Dead Man ' at Fertun . . . another cheery spot . . . we hadn't had bite nor sup between our teeth for five days . . . my belly fairly howled. . . . But that was nothing compared to the thirst. . . . Taught one a lot of queer dodges, that did. . . ."

Hiesinger only nodded at this topical reminiscence.

Conversation flagged.

In the dwindling daylight, two fairly strong detachments advanced on the pillbox but were held up by its fire about ten paces away from the block of cement.

Gunner Scharf, who had played an active part in repulsing the attack, then reported that the water in the jacket was giving out and, as regards ammunition, the last two belts had been brought out.

Something would have to be done.

The pillbox party did not dare to rely exclusively on the relief due after midnight.

Lieutenant Goebel discussed the position with the N.C.O.

"You'll have to go back, Corporal . . . must at all costs restore communications."

The corporal did not like the errand much. He raised objections and then fell back on his destroyed orders.

The lieutenant looked at Schmalz firmly, but with no unfriendly gaze.

"Now look here, Corporal Schmalz . . . I don't want to start by pointing out that I am in command of this strong point. . . . I quite understand that you want to stand by your men and I respect you for it. . . . You are doing it from a sense of comradeship. . . . But as things are, you will prove your comradeship best by bringing up relief as quickly as possible. . . . You know well enough how matters stand and what we are short of. . . ."

The lieutenant's last hint was not lost on the N.C.O., but he hesitated still.

"I suppose you couldn't detach someone else, sir? . . . I should like to be here to hand over."

Lieutenant Goebel understood the reason for the refusal, which in fact, was none, because in accordance with his orders, the corporal was only trying to hold his post until relieved and, strictly speaking, it was his duty to hold it. He gripped the N.C.O.'s arm lightly:

"You go back, Corporal, and report the state of things at the pillbox. . . . I don't want to send anyone else. . . . And, since you attach so much importance to orders in writing, I am going to give you a written order that will leave no room for doubt why you left the pillbox before being relieved. . . ."

Without another word, the N.C.O. gave in.

The lieutenant took a dispatch block from his wallet and wrote out the promised instructions by the dim light of a candle. Then he unfolded a map of the battle sector and beckoned to the corporal to come closer.

With their heads together, officer and N.C.O. pored over the map. The maze of strokes and lines was not altogether easy to disentangle. The lieutenant's finger followed one or two markings and came to a standstill at a point marked with a red cross.

136

"That ought to be Pillbox 17, Corporal.
. . . We're in advance of our front line. . . .
That is the forward artillery line and this—
make a good note of the lie of it—is Sector
headquarters. . . . It's about a kilometre
away from here, or a bit less. . . . I can't tell
you how the several lines are held. . . . The
map shows the order of battle as it was at noon
yesterday. . . . In the interval things may
have changed a good deal. . . . Yes, if only
that communication trench were clear still.
. . . So far as one can get the hang of things
it will be best for you to make your way to
the artillery lines, that is to say, straight
back. . . . It won't be easy going, Corporal. . . . Take a trustworthy man with
you. . . ."

The N.C.O. considered rapidly whom he
could take. Scharf? No, that wouldn't do.
Scharf was the only fully trained M.G. marksman. Biegler, the pillbox infant? He was
not looking well and had not had enough experience. So there was only Nuetzel left and the
corporal left it at that.

It was in no sense of the word a picnic that
they had in prospect. But Nuetzel behaved as
if it were a Sunday outing. The prospect of

scrounging something to drink put him in the best of spirits.

In a few minutes the two messengers on whose pluck and resourcefulness the fate of the pillbox hung, were ready to set out.

Corporal Schmalz borrowed the map from the lieutenant and initiated Nuetzel into the mysteries of its strokes and whorls.

Time pressed.

Lieutenant Goebel patted the corporal's shoulder:

"I am counting on you with every confidence, Corporal Schmalz. . . . To-morrow evening about this time, at latest. . . . You must have good luck, for your luck is our luck. . . . See you again to-morrow evening, then! . . ."

The whole pillbox party crowded round Nuetzel and the corporal. Everyone shook hands with them, Scharf after quite a noticeably long grip of the N.C.O.'s hand, and Hiesinger delivered the farewell address.

"Come back soon, both of you. . . . So that our family party is kept up at full strength and moves into billets as a unit . . . and bring back something to drink. . . . The more the merrier. . . ."

138

Everyone cheered the request with enthusiasm. Even the Canadian tapped his
throat with the gesture of one manipulating
a bottle.

Once more Corporal Schmalz looked round
the pillbox. He took leave of each article
severally. At the last, his glance fell on his
old battered spirit cooker.

Then he called to Nuetzel.

The two men slipped out of the pillbox.

¶ Stalking by Moonlight.
¶ Interlude at the Crater.

THE night, bright and hot, spread over the crater-field. Star strung to star made a necklet of pearls and decked night's brow in the lofty vault of a serene sky.

Corporal Schmalz and Nuetzel were not in the least enraptured by the beauty of the night.

Was the moon bound to shine at this particular juncture, as if she were being paid overtime?

In this light every object threw a trebly enlarged shadow. Nuetzel and the N.C.O., however, took no pleasure in seeing their shadows or in allowing them to be seen.

They had succeeded in slipping out of the pillbox although the enemy outpost was only ten paces away. He no doubt must have been of a romantic disposition because he saw and heard nothing.

Behind the pillbox, trouble began.

Only a mole could have burrowed its way through the brightness unobserved and even a mole would not have enjoyed the task, so horribly did the place stink.

It was not for nothing that the sun had been scorching down on the crater-field all day long. The lightest breath of air bore odours that bred nausea, a stench of death brewed of all the juices of putrefaction.

A wave of fragrance of this sort that brought nausea nearer them than any preceding wave, passed over them at that very moment.

Where was the dead horse that gave the misery of the innocent animal world such penetrating expression?

The noisome wave assailed the corporal's nose somewhere from the right. The advance artillery line must therefore lie in that direction.

Yard by yard they propelled themselves into the crater-field, always keeping the direction of the stench of the dead horse. As a sign-post it was more trustworthy than any map. At times they hardly knew which way to turn their head, so unbearable was the reek.

They had left the pillbox a hundred yards behind them. They were bound to strike the first line soon.

Nuetzel, crawling noiselessly beside the

corporal, suddenly sagged into the earth. Involuntarily the N.C.O. followed his lead. They were lying in a shallow scoop, apparently the remnant of a wrecked sap. Not twenty paces away a figure came in sight, or really only half a figure, for from the hips downwards the man was in a trench. The flat steel helmet and the fact that his back was turned to them, told them all they needed to know.

The first line was occupied by the others. Whether in whole or in part or to what extent, was the problem. There was nothing to be gathered from the gunfire. It was the customary harassing fire.

Turn back? Not on any account.

They had to get through. There would be a loophole somewhere or other.

The corporal crawled a few yards back and then dragged himself to the right. The trench was bound to come to an end somewhere and the outpost would be outflanked.

But this end appeared to lie far out in the night. For half an hour or more they squirmed along behind the occupied line. Another outpost. . . . Yet another. . . . A third.

The only luck about it was that they did not lose the putrid trail of the dead horse. They still held on in the main direction.

They allowed themselves a few minutes' easy to regain their breath in a crater.

Nuetzel shook the beads of sweat from his forehead and whispered in the corporal's ear:

"Three weeks ago we were in line here . . . a very windy bit of line, Corporal. . . . I remember it pretty well. . . . If I am not altogether wrong, we are a bit too far right as it is. . . . Near the last outpost there ought to be a sap. . . . Whether it is there still not even G.H.Q. knows."

The corporal digested this information.

"Too far right, you think? . . . I'm inclined to think so myself now . . . the trench can't be as long as all that. . . . So let us wriggle forward a bit. . . . Somewhere or other the plumber's bound to have left a hole."

A machine-gun bleated away and striped the darkness blood red. The flash of the discharge was in clear view.

Nuetzel followed the track of the flash with his eyes.

"Now I know where I am, Corporal. . . . That gun is mounted on our old emplacement.

. . . Close to it the trench runs out. . . .
There used to be a pretty fair gap to the next
trench there. We shall run our heads into it if
we keep straight ahead. . . ."

The situation was for the first time being
cleared up. They held straight on and soon
came upon the barbed wire entanglement. The
belt was broad and deep and necessitated a
wide sweep to the right. At length they
reached the gap, of which Nuetzel had spoken.

But what was that?

A clang and a clink, dumping and dull
thuds, such as are occasioned when the sods of
soil are being thrown up, resounded through
the night.

Both men held their breath.

Someone was digging in quite near them, to
judge by the sound, in the gap between the
wire. But who was it digging, their own
people or the others?

At first it was impossible to make out
anything. But after the eye had become
accustomed to the peculiar light, the corporal
distinguished the digging party. They had
already trenched themselves in up to their
knees and were throwing out the soil in front
of themselves.

That put an end to doubt. The occupied line was being extended and the gap between the trenches closed up.

It would be, so the corporal estimated, about fifty yards from the spot where they were lying to the first of the trenching party.

They had, at all risks, to get through here, otherwise the night would be spent and they would still be lying on the wrong side of the occupied line.

So there was not much time left for deliberation. Every spadeful thrown up was narrowing the gap and thereby lessening the prospects of slipping through.

Ear to ear the corporal conferred with Nuetzel.

"We've got to get through, Nuetzel. . . . Or they'll bag us as soon as the night is over. But we'll have to sprint like the devil. . . . If they should drop me, don't you bother about it. . . . Carry on. . . . Our pals are waiting."

Nuetzel was not, it is true, a man of many or deep thoughts, but he was, to make up for it, as resolute, active, and tough a fellow as any other. He whispered back: "I'm with you, Corporal. . . . Going through them, be sure to follow your nose. . . . Don't, for the Lord's sake, bear to the left. . . . Else we shall hang ourselves up in the wire. . . . For all I care we may as well kick off."

But first of all they stole their way up to a level with the night working party and there gathered their strength for the dash for life or death.

The man in the chain working nearest to the wire, no doubt hardly trusted his eyes. Were they playing him false?

Two shadows were speeding through the clear night.

The pounding of heavy boots startled the man out of his amazement.

"Halt, there. . . . Halt!"

He threw away his spade, snatched up his rifle, and loosed a couple of shots in the wake of the shadows.

The noise of the shots roused the lines. On either side wild rifle fire ran up and down the trenches. Nuetzel and the corporal were on the far side of the wire. They squeezed themselves, panting, into the ground. Every pulse was racing at the double. Pressed flat as they could flatten themselves, they gasped for want of breath. Crimson veils bemused their brain.

146

But their luck held.

The report of shots had made the German lines alert. Heavy firing blazed up and poured into the gap beyond the wire. Over Nuetzel and the corporal's heads, German steel-nosed bullets buzzed angrily. They enfiladed the trenching party and drove them back to cover.

The fusillade lasted a full quarter of an hour, and then, but for isolated shots, died down.

Cautiously the N.C.O. raised his head.

They were lying in No Man's Land, in an open field between the trenches. The wire was clearly outlined in the moonlight. They could not stay there long without being discovered.

They moved on sinuously and covered fifty yards on their bellies—only to sight an outpost at ten paces distant. The flat steel helmet again and the face turned away from the two stalkers.

The corporal's hand stole to his belt and unhooked a stick bomb, as Nuetzel noted in a twinkling and followed his example.

One more step and one more. . . . Now! The N.C.O. hurled his bomb from a half crouching attitude.

At the roar of the explosion both men were

on their feet and dashed on in long bounds, straight into the witch's cauldron.

From three directions artillery and rifle fire flayed the ground. They had jarred a sensitive nerve of the front line.

Nuetzel felt a violent blow in his knee, swore under his breath and of a sudden had an impression that his left leg must be composed of solid lead.

They crawled to a crater and dived into it. This crater was a pit of hellish stench—the reek of it was unspeakable.

The corporal trod on some soft object. Under his weight the object gave way and half way up his leg he was standing in slimy ooze. The dead horse!

In the effort to drag his leg out of the corpse, the N.C.O. trod on a human foot. He felt the shape of it through the sole of his boot. Then nature had its revenge.

He was as sick as a dog.

The main point was: they were through and out of the zone of fire. That was worth the libation offered which in any case did not amount to much.

Nuetzel was cursing as his spirit gave him utterance.

148

" Cursed mess up. . . . Plunk into the left knee. . . . Couldn't the blasted fool have kept it a hand's breadth lower down. . . . Then it would have passed through the calf and I should have got away with it cheap. . . ."

The bullet had shattered Nuetzel's left knee-cap. Nuetzel was sitting beside the corporal and slitting up trouser leg and top boot.

" As regards carrying on, there's nothing doing, Corporal. . . . The leg looks to me as rotten as a horse-radish in August. . . . And I'm damned if I don't believe that one of our crowd planted that bullet on me. . . . That's the sort of idiot that's still about after three years of the war. . . ."

Growling and cursing, Nuetzel pulled out his roll of dressing. The corporal contributed his and tied a tight bandage round the shattered knee. While doing so, he incidentally wiped the perspiration from his face and noticed blood on his right hand. Until then, he had not been aware of the slight graze on his neck.

Rifle fire still went on in nervous spasms through the night, but gradually died down.

Corporal Schmalz lugged out the grandfather watch and held it close up to his eyes.

Incredible! They had been on the move for four hours. . . . It was close on two o'clock and that was borne out by the position of the stars. So it was high time to push on. They were sure to be counting every minute in the pillbox.

Nuetzel seemed to divine his thoughts.

"Get on with it on your own, Corporal. . . . It can't be very far now. . . . I'll squat in the crater here and wait till they send to bring me in. . . . You won't forget me, Corporal, will you? . . . And tell the plaster monger that I should like something to drink . . . and no short measure. . . . I'd prefer a bucket to a thimbleful. . . ."

An irrepressible fellow, Nuetzel. The corporal shook him by the hand.

"You can bank on it, Nuetzel. . . . I'll send out the first one I get hold of. . . . I reckon we are close to the advance artillery line. . . . They won't be short of Medical Service people there. . . . And where there're Medical orderlies, schnaps won't be far off."

One more hard grip of the hands, a reciprocal pat on the back and the N.C.O. disappeared out of the crater.

Nuetzel lay back against the slope and tried to sleep.

While he crept away crouched up, to fling himself flat on his face at every sound, the corporal visualized the map of the position from memory. Beside this map, Lieutenant Goebel's narrow, self-controlled face persisted in appearing. What were things like in Pillbox 17? Was the pillbox there at all by this time?

After half an hour's stalking, Schmalz caught his foot in a trip wire. So he knew his whereabouts.

The advanced artillery line of the sector followed the slight rise of some sand dunes. It became possible to make shelters and funkholes here which offered better cover than the dugouts built up of sandbags and hurdles of the lower lying area.

At the very first dug-out, Schmalz fell in with a first-aid station. He described the way to Dead Horse crater to the stretcher bearer carefully and more especially impressed Nuetzel's thirst upon him.

The honest fellow first expressed, at some length, his amazement at the state of affairs outlined, and then had a long pull at his water bottle. Nuetzel might feel assured of meeting with sympathetic understanding from this quarter where drink was concerned.

After he felt justified in believing that his friend would be looked after, Schmalz did not cut any more time to waste.

The advanced artillery line was connected with the battle Sector H.Q. by a direct communication trench. It was none the less unpleasant going, consisting as it did for the most part of shell holes and it was being handsomely sprayed.

It took the corporal a good hour before he had picked his way through the communication trench. The Headquarters dug-out was buzzing like a beehive. Messengers and runners crowded the entrance. Every man held his own particular dispatch to be the most urgent. The field telephone was buzzing incessantly. In front of it sat a black-haired giant of a captain, chewing a cigar end. The captain was a model of composure. With the headpiece of the telephone over his ears he was scribbling furiously on a block of forms, transferring the stale remnant of his cigar from one corner of his mouth to the other the while. Without interrupting the diverse occupations of

152

listening and scribbling for a moment, he scanned the reports as they came in as well.

After he had glanced at Lieutenant Goebel's report on the conditions of Pillbox 17, the captain removed his headpiece. He went on playing with his cigar end unmoved and shrugged his shoulders lightly.

"Nothing doing before nightfall, Corporal. Is it really as bad as all that up there?"

In concise words, Corporal Schmalz reported all there was to report on the situation at Pillbox 17. He did not omit to stress the lieutenant's wound.

The gigantic captain listened unmoved.

"Sounds like bad business. . . . But there's nothing doing before dark. . . . Until then, the people in the pillbox will have to stick it. . . . . You keep somewhere near me, Corporal. There'll probably be room in the adjoining dug-out. . . ."

Schmalz came to attention with a click of his heels.

"Very good, sir. . . . In the adjoining dug-out. . . ."

There was room in the dug-out. Schmalz found some old acquaintances among its occupants, too. But first of all he drank his fill.

Nuetzel, about the same time, was doing the same thing. They had succeeded in bringing him in before daylight. He was now sitting on a bunk in the First Aid dug-out, and was just sampling the sixth brand of schnaps.

The trial was eminently satisfactory so far as both Nuetzel and the schnaps were concerned.

¶ Buried—The Light goes Out.

AT 2.11 p.m. a flat trajectory shell hit Pillbox 17 and tilted it half over.

The shell burst immediately in front of the pillbox and bored its way beneath the foundations. It left the cement column itself undamaged, but the force of the explosion and the air pressure were strong enough to cause the shelter to sag over to one side.

A shattering roar resounded through the pillbox and even before it had died away men and things were tumbled over in wild confusion. A tangle of heads, feet, arms and packs followed the explosion. Plank beds, ammunition boxes and machine-gun parts were turned topsyturvy.

It was some time before the tangle sorted itself out. There were no casualties, only the volunteer had a scalp wound inflicted by the hard floor. Lieutenant Goebel came crawling on all fours out of the corner, into which he had rolled, and behind him, the tall Canadian hauled himself to his feet. There was a hint of pallor on the officer's face, but his voice was as steady and controlled as ever.

"Fall in, everyone. . . . Keep your heads, men. . . . The shelter, you see, is still quite intact."

That was a fact.

But Scharf, who had been examining the emplacement, reported that the gun was out of action because it was half-buried in the ground.

Much more serious was the news that the Red Cross lance-corporal, Hiesinger, reported.

"Sir . . . the entrance is buried."

Inspection showed that the entrance was sunk into the soil. The tilt of the pillbox was backwards. One man looked at the other without a word. A numbing silence fell over the shelter.

Lieutenant Goebel drew in his lower lip and studied the tip of his boots.

"Keep your tails up, men . . . no harm done, so far. . . . The entrance will have to be cleared . . . every man lend a hand. . . . Scharf and Biegler will dig on the right, the lance-corporal and the man from Canada on the left of the spot where we can look to strike the entrance. . . . Half-hour shifts."

After the departure of the corporal and Nuetzel, the garrison of No. 17 still amounted to seven men and the Canadian. In addition to these, the three stragglers who had come in that morning, including the wounded man.

In the background, against the cement wall, with his right arm extended stiffly from his body, straddled the dead man.

They dug in and shovelled on either side of the body. The Canadian displayed such keenness and skill that he soon left all the rest a long way behind him. The man knew all there was to know about handling pick and shovel.

Only rarely did a spoken word break the monotonous sounds of scraping and dumping.

Even in this anxious state of affairs, Hiesinger kept true to type.

He watched the work of his partner from Canada with approval and, since there was no point in talking to the man in khaki, gave tongue to Scharf:

"Chap knows his job . . . must have had a lot to do with pick and shovel, eh, 'cause it comes sort of natural to him? . . . Should say he must be a farmer or something of that sort. . . ."

Scharf nodded indifferently in response to

these speculations. The sticky heat of the pill-box was becoming harder and harder to bear. The arid spectre of thirst was silently going the rounds.

They had already relieved shifts three times, but the entrance remained swallowed up in the earth and refused to be cleared.

The Red Cross man drew himself up exhausted and rubbed the small of his aching back. Wiping his spade, he noticed that the earth sticking to it, was very moist.

He went on digging furiously and every now and then picked up a sample of the soil which he felt to be cool and damp against his hand. He shouted for a candle and threw the light into the hole he had dug.

A dull grey eye blinked at the bottom of it. Surface water. Drop by drop it sickered up and trickled out of the sides. Hiesinger wriggled out of the hole and went up to the lieutenant.

"We have struck water, sir. . . . No damn good going on digging there. . . ."

The news set the pillbox abuzz.

Water!

Only a word to the ears of the man who has never had to do without water, but a miracle for the men who had been tortured by thirst for hours, a blessing of life, full of promise, allurement, and comfort.

Lieutenant Goebel understood what they felt.

"We're in luck's way, boys . . . or don't you call it luck to strike water all of a sudden? . . . Go on digging cautiously and be careful not to spill more soil into it than you can help."

The lieutenant was well aware of the doom louring behind this stroke of luck. For the appearance of percolating water showed that the prospect of a way into the open was barred at this spot.

Four mugs containing a muddy fluid were the yield of long hours of digging.

Hiesinger, as the discoverer, was allowed to do the honours. He first served the lieutenant who drank the same ration allotted to the rest of the party—half a mug per head. Then the Red Cross man poured out rather more than their fair share for the wounded and contented himself with the smaller portion remaining.

Nor was the man from Canada left out. He took the mug, but first raised his hand to a helmet that was not there, and then drained the brew with a grin.

The few drops of dirty water revived the spirit of hopefulness. A wave of cheerfulness and confidence passed through the half over-turned cement pillar.

The Red Cross man was already considering the chances of relief and was expounding them to the others.

" The corporal's got through . . . my little finger tells me so. . . . And, as he's through, then he'll get us out of the schemozzel . . . that is as certain as the clerk saying Amen to the parson. . . . Our corporal won't let go there. . . . He'll go straight through to Army H.Q. if need be."

Scharf seconded the confidence in the N.C.O. with unreserved conviction.

Hiesinger went on:

" It'll be dark in four hours' time . . . if nothing more happens till then we've won through. . . . Bet the corporal's sitting on needles. . . . I know him well enough for that. . . . If he could wangle it, there wouldn't be any daylight at all. . . . That's the sort of fellow he is. . . ."

The man who sang this simple song of com-radeship-in-arms was no seer, nor more of a poet than is every human being by nature.

160

He was a hard, half-starved, front line foot-slogger, without nerves. But his heart saw things in their true light. . . .

Half a rifle shot in the rear, Corporal Schmalz was pacing the dug-out. Every other minute he had to make sure that it was still broad daylight. He bit through the mouth-piece of his pipe in his impatience.

The men in the pillbox could not see this impatience with their eyes, but something of this restlessness infected them. Hiesinger pulled at his fingers until the joints cracked audibly.

"If it'ud only get dark. . . . The corporal can't come before. . . . I am reckoning on about nine, they'll be here by ten o'clock. . . . Then, it's true, they'll have to dig for another three or four hours. . . ."

Lieutenant Goebel nodded encouragement to the lance-corporal.

"Once they've started digging we've won through. . . . We'll dig to meet them. . . . It'll take half the time that way. . . ."

All expressed their resolve to dig as they had never dug before.

A little after four o'clock in the afternoon, a second shell wedged Pillbox 17 completely

L   161 into the ground. This shell had arrived slant-wise and gave the column a twist. The observation slit and the firing embrasure were now earthed up as well.

Eight human beings were plunged into the earth as though in a diving bell; except that there was no pump to bring in the air from above.

A hope that the second hit might have cleared the entrance was soon dead and buried.

The block of cement was as if soldered up. Two candles were burning dim and quite rigid and only flickered their flame when an exhalation of breath caught them.

Grey sweat beaded every forehead; horror and dawning madness glowered in many an eye. There was no need to waste words on the state of things. Every man understood the end of it.

They all huddled close round the bunks and stared past one another. In the case of one man there might have been a chance of escape. In the case of eight men there was no such chance. One man was robbing the other of air, a heavy, stale air, weighing on chest and head, as if it were compounded of cement.

162

They were murdering one another in shifts. They realised it, too, and only had ceased to have the strength to follow their unreasoning hate.

Madness broke out in Scharf first.

With the howl of a wolf he leapt up, seized a trenching tool, and hammered away at the cement wall. The spade shivered to splinters but the man went on hammering away with fists and feet. Foam was dripping from his mouth and his shriek, with the death rattle in it: "Get out, there. Get out," was ghastly.

Scharf drummed against the grey, merciless wall until blood spurted from his fists. At last he ran his head against it. Then, streaming with blood, he collapsed and remained lying on his face, motionless.

By this time it had gripped the next. He was Hicsinger's sharp-tongued challenger. His attack was only short-lived. He lacked Scharf's splendid physique.

The air became thick and foul. They seemed to be breathing slime. Their heads dropped lower and lower. It was only with difficulty that they kept their eyes open.

Biegler, the volunteer, leaned back, squatting against an empty ammunition box. His faery eyes stood out blue and big in the dim candle light.

What was it these eyes were gazing at?

A little house in the suburbs . . . fuchsias and geraniums in the window boxes . . . a motherly woman with a kindly smile was just coming out of the door. . . . Wonder how old mother is? . . . She must surely always have been alive and would go on living to all eternity. . . . In the attic his studio . . . the easel . . . the pot for brushes . . . the brown, wooden frames. . . .

Visions of this simple, happy life closed round the dying painter, they dangled to and fro before his eyes and led him away, away out of the grey desolation of the shelter that had become a coffin.

Biegler's lips moved voicelessly.

"Though I pass through . . . the valley of darkness . . . I fear no evil . . . for Thou art with me . . . Thy rod and Thy staff . . . they comfort me."

At the volunteer's side, with an arm flung round Biegler's shoulders, the tall Canadian was breathing in gasps. He was rocking his head to and fro and oddly foreign, yet familiar

164

words took shape through the laboured rattle of his breathing.

The Canadian was singing a song of his far-off mighty native land, he hummed it in a hoarse, breaking voice and Biegler, leaning against the Canadian's shoulder, heard words that seemed to come from the depths of a dream.

> *In our village,*
> *Fly, my heart, fly,*
> *In our village,*
> *Dwelt two sisters.*
>
> *The one was brown,*
> *Fly, my heart, fly,*
> *The one was brown,*
> *Fair was the other.*

The words came softly and ran out in murmurs and gasps.

Boundless expanses of prairie, a village of brown shacks, immeasurable forests, passed before the young painter's vision and in that vision his fainting soul passed in silence with the soul of that other.

It was dark by this time outside, and in the darkness fierce fighting for the lost crater line was raging.

165

The German counter attack set in so hotly and so unexpectedly that in less than a quarter-of-an-hour it had swept over the old front line.

Corporal Schmalz advanced with the spear-head troops. He had been in a fever of impatience all the afternoon and was now like a very drunken man. With three sappers he was hunting for the vanished pillbox.

Lieutenant Goebel never guessed that only twenty paces away rescue was at hand. The N.C.O. was following the battered communication trench and now felt sure of finding the pillbox at the next step or two.

His mouth twisted in torment, the lieutenant was lying at the foot of the plank bed. Two long legs dangled beside him. He had ceased to be aware that they were the legs of the Red Cross lance-corporal.

Knives were probing his lungs. Every intake of breath was a dagger's thrust.

Fiery lights were dancing in his brain and luring him back into the past.

Had it been yesterday that he had entrained with the regiment?

Surely, that was Clara, his betrothed, standing there waving her hand to him?

No. . . . It wasn't Clara. It was his best

pal who had fallen on that beautiful May morning on one of the slopes behind Arras. . . .

Outside, the N.C.O. had found the overturned pillbox. Dumbly he stared at the smooth grey cement wall that returned his gaze, dully, cruelly. . . .

Within, the last candle was burning dimly. It was only half burnt out but its light was being stifled slowly, just as the men whose death agony it had lit up, had been suffocated.

Lieutenant Goebel fought with the last of his strength for the wretched remnant of air, still possible to breathe in the stifling atmosphere of reeking stench. He watched the flame of the candle fighting for its ebbing life.

Before the last light was wholly extinct and his own consciousness left him, the lieutenant drew his automatic. It seemed to him as if he had to lift a hundredweight of steel to his temples.

Two shots rang out. . . . A weakly body sank back on the boards of the plank bed.

Lieutenant Goebel's shots, turned against himself, were the last signs of life from Pillbox No. 17.

¶ Salving the Bodies.
¶ The Story of Madlon.

FOR two hours the sappers had been working for all their muscles were worth.

The outlines of the pillbox had gradually emerged from the ground, but the hole of entry remained earthed up.

Corporal Schmalz dug in the foremost line. He wielded the heavy sapper's spade with a strength and endurance that earned him the respect and admiration of his fellow workers.

But the corporal was not in the least concerned with that. He was only goaded by one thought: "Hurry . . . hurry, I have to get them out alive."

He worked like a maniac and urged on the men who did not want any urging. Every man knew what was at stake. Five minutes won, that might mean snatching eight human lives from under the skeleton arm of Death, the destroyer.

All round them the noise of battle clattered. No one paid any heed to it.

168

At length they came a big step nearer their objective. A sapper had struck the sole of the trench. By digging along the bottom of the trench they were bound to find the pillbox entry.

It was not to be done as quickly and simply as the corporal's consuming impatience could have hoped, although after half-an-hour's record labour, the spades were ringing against the cement.

The second hit had given the pillar a twist. The entrance opening had therefore bored into the side of the trench and was not lying directly in the line of the communication trench.

They now attacked the parados. They shovelled the soil upwards from the sole of the trench.

In his heart the corporal had hoped that the pillbox party would dig to meet them. He had pictured in his mind's eye how he would address Lance-Corporal Hiesinger or Gunner Scharf or whoever else might be the first to crawl out of the pillbox, in a feigned voice. He even now had this game of hide and seek in his mind, but he had no real faith in his make-believe.

The pillbox was lying as grey and aloof in front of his as a primeval drift rock left behind by a sea that had vanished ages ago. Schmalz struck the cement with a trenching iron. But no sound other than the reverberations of the blow responded.

His heart throbbed the ghastly truth with every beat and yet refused to accept is as the truth.

His comrades could surely only be unconscious and that was the reason why they failed to respond. Of course they were unconscious. What else could they be?

When, at what hour would they have been buried? Important to know that. Three hours or twelve hours ago?

Amid these thoughts the corporal went on throwing up the earth. The balls of his hands burnt like fire. At a thrust of the iron, the spade suddenly met with no resistance. Corporal Schmalz drove into the hole up to his shoulder blade.

Ten minutes later the pillbox entry was clear.

Everyone listened intently, whether they could not catch a sound, a sob or a groan.

Not a sound . . . not a movement . . . not a sign of life.

Corporal Schmalz stared at the familiar pill-box hole. It surely could not be. Deathly silence gaped from the interior.

Schmalz shook off the sense of dizziness and bent down to crawl into the pillbox.

Someone was lying straight across the entry and barred admission.

The sappers dragged the body out. It was the abdominal bullet wound, the only soul in the pillbox who had been spared the hour of the last horror.

A small searchlight lit up the interior with a glare.

Corporal Schmalz stood at the entrance and moved the light to and fro from one corner to the other mechanically. The toes of his boots were almost touching two figures lying crumpled up in front of them.

The corporal's head sank on his chest. For minutes that later became imprinted on the memory as eternities, he never moved a muscle. A comrade was taking leave of his comrades-in-arms. His rigid posture was a voiceless night parade.

"Get on with it, Corporal. . . . We have

got to get back . . . the Division's being pulled out to-night. . . ."

The sapper's voice roused the corporal.

Once more he looked round the pillbox.

Those two, one with his head on the shoulder of the other, were Biegler, the pillbox infant, and the tall fellow from Canada.

Across the lower bunk lay Lieutenant Goebel, clutching his automatic in his clenched right hand.

The legs dangling from the upper bunk were those of Lance-Corporal Hiesinger of the Army Medical Service. Hiesinger's head was bedded below the heart of the man with the shot wound in his chest, as if even at the point of death the Red Cross man were tending the wounded.

Corporal Schmalz bent over the figures at his feet and flashed the light on them.

Scharf, his old pal, and the newcomer with the subtle tongue.

And dead, all of them dead.

Was not he, Corporal Alois Schmalz, guilty of their deaths? Ought he not to have stayed behind and shared the end with his comrades-in-arms? Why had he not come to their aid earlier?

The N.C.O. passed his hand across his forehead.

"It's all such damned foolery. . . ." the sappers hear him mutter.

Wrapped up in ground sheets, the dead were brought out and carried to the rear.

Schmalz was the last of the party to leave the pillbox. He dug out the buried machine-gun and humped it on his shoulders. But he first gave the gun a savage kick and added, "Cursed sausage machine".

The Division was being taken out of the line. Ever since night had fallen, reliefs were being effected.

Schmalz had beaten up some men of his company. With their aid he succeeded in taking the dead of Pillbox 17 over the three kilometres back to rest billets. They were laid out side by side in a barn.

Another day was close at hand, yet men of the company, singly or in groups, kept coming into the barn. They discussed what had happened in whispers.

"Pity about Lieutenant Goebel . . . but that kind never lasts long. . . . Others whom one'd miss less, turn up at mess. . . ."

"The tall blighter, the Red Cross Schnaps,

used to gas, it's true, till he gave you a belly ache. . . . Otherwise, he was a first-class chap. . . ."

"It was on the Tuesday that chap Scharf says to me: 'Lutz,' he says, 'you damn well see that there's beer handy when we come out of the schemozzel'. . . . That's what he says and the beer's there all right . . . now he can't drink another one . . . that chap Scharf, and he fair loved it. . . . Dog's life."

"I'm awfully sorry about him, the little artist fellow. . . . Such a quiet, decent little chap."

Every man had a kindly word to say and every epilogue came from an honest heart.

Corporal Schmalz had his billet close to the barn. He was dog tired but did not like to lie down because another duty stood between him and rest.

The packs of his dead comrades-in-arms were stacked round him. He had searched their bodies, too, and had had everything belonging to them to his room.

The company was quartered some five kilometres further in the rear.

Sergeant-Major Schinzel would undoubtedly have no objection to raise if Corporal Schmalz relieved him of the job.

The N.C.O.'s rough, knotted fingers sorted a quaint trove of letters, photographs, pencils, bits of fuse and all the oddments that link the soldier in the line with life. Schmalz was careful to see that every trifle was allocated to its right pile. His initial hesitation to examine things more closely to glance at letters, to look at pictures, soon disappeared.

The young lady with the merry smile was Lieutenant Goebel's fiancée. Wonder whether she will go on smiling like that when. . . .

In a letter scrawled in pencil by Scharf the N.C.O. read: "Our corporal, his name is Schmalz, is a topping fellow. . . ."

Corporal Schmalz put the letter on one side quickly and couldn't understand why his eyes suddenly began to smart.

The possessions of Biegler, the Pillbox infant, gave him most trouble. Schmalz was astonished by the number of sketches hurriedly dashed off in pencil. How had Biegler found time for them? It was against orders to make sketches. A faded sheet of an old Army newspaper fell into the corporal's hands. A column or so of the sheet was framed in red pencil.

Schmalz began to read. This is the short story he read:

MADLON

"When we entered Bonviller that evening, half the hamlet was in ruins. The stars looked down into the stinking cow stall in which we were billetted and the moon at times pressed her round, chubby face inquisitively through the shattered roof. But she always retired again quickly for we were all lying snoring on our stomachs. Moon and stars might well be fond of us and God the Father and all the archangels thrown in, for all we cared.

"None of us savoured of roses the next morning. With the cow feathers still in our hair and on our tunics, we pervaded the wretched village street in quest of something hot to drink. The stomach is the soldier's sternest commanding officer, and enthusiasm has never yet stilled a hungry man's hunger.

"In front of a comparatively habitable farmhouse, half the Company had assembled. A woman was reported to be making coffee there and to be selling it at twopence a cup. Whether the coffee was the attraction or the woman, any way, there was a squash as there no doubt will be on the Last Day when there is a ration issue of eternal salvation.

"The darkish room was fairly bursting with soldiers. Where there was only room for two seats, four squeezed in. Soldiers crowded round the table, in front of the stove, behind a bench and between two beds behind a screen. The three available chairs provided accommodation for seven occupants. Everyone was blowing the boiling brew with inflated cheeks and sipping it out of mess-tin lids with pursed lips.

" Then the door opened and Madlon came in.

" A murmur, a low buzz, came in from the street along the dark passage with her. Her slimness of seventeen swayed on rounded hips and under her blue shapeless smock her young breasts responded to her every step.

" We had had no chance of a change for five days and looked as if we had been in a trench grave for twice as long. Yesterday, woman and the world had been wiped out of our memory and if anyone had begun to talk of love we should have jeered at him.

" And now, some fifty men were pecking and preening themselves like hens with an attack of mites. One squinted at the other sideways and rejoiced if the other looked still more unwashed. All for the sake of Madlon who, slender and unruffled, passed through the room and never looked at a single man.

" We were quartered in Bonviller until the following afternoon. Not far in front of us the shell-bursts were spurting high as a house into the September sky. We neither saw nor heard anything of them. The war had sunk a hundred thousand fathoms underground. The earth flowered like a garden of peace all round us.

"The room at Mother Rambouillet's was full to overflowing at any hour of the day. All of them soldiers athirst for coffee. Many a man did his twenty cups. Madlon stood at the stove and the open log fire flickered in her dark, unmoved, virginal face. Hundreds of male eyes followed Madlon's every movement and revelled in them. Mother Rambouillet thought it timely to let it be known that Madlon's betrothed had been called up to the dragoons in Toul. It only invested the girl with new allurement.

"Madlon no doubt realized that she was the focus of a fiery ring of desire. Many a quick glance aimed at her under lowered lids, betrayed it. But she only laughed a deep, cooing laugh at all the compliments showered upon her, though often enough they were on the emphatic side.

"Every man wooed her after his own fashion. One man tenderly and respectfully, another roughly and clumsily like a puppy.

"For thirty blessed hours we breathed the fragrance of life and almost forgot how musty is the reek of death. One man watched his fellow and all watched over Madlon, who could not move a step without drawing a bodyguard of twenty men in her train. A weirder game has never been played. All were driven by the like desire but, because everyone shared that desire, no one dared do more than crave. We should have done any

man in out of hand who had dared to lay even a
finger on Madlon.

"Then we moved up into line. It was all that
was to be expected of it.

"Close beside us the latrine reeked to heaven."

On the margin of the sheet Biegler had
some pencil studies: a few men in field grey,
sipping coffee, a capacious matron, probably
honest Mother Rambouillet, and in many
poses a girl's dainty head, portraying Madlon.

Corporal Schmalz studied the drawings
closely. He was not a great art critic, but he
became conscious of the love and reverence
which differentiated these sketches from reminiscence of a day's leave from the line.

Bonviller? . . . Mother Rambouillet? . . .
The girl Madlon? . . . The coffee parade?
. . . Of course. . . . He, too, knew all
about that—

Corporal Schmalz felt the war-time clock
being put back by two years. He brooded
over it and knocked out his pipe.

Wasn't Scharf one of the party at the time?
. . . And Nuetzel. . . . And. . . . And. . . .

The shadows of dead comrades-in-arms rose
up and saluted the lonely man in the night.

What made him do it he was never really

able to explain to himself. But Corporal Schmalz wrote on the empty margin under the sketch of Madlon, in big, clumsy letters: "That is true. . . . Was there in Bonviller myself."

The attempt to fill another pipe failed. With his arms spread wide over the table, the N.C.O. fell asleep.

It was his fourth night without sleep.

¶ At the Sign of the Seven Sisters.
¶ The Blow in the Face.

SERGEANT-MAJOR SCHINZEL did not smoke good stuff, he was an old regular and just before the outbreak of war had become ripe for the appointment of usher to the County Court. After two and twenty years service, pretty well all the secrets of military activity were an open book to him.

So far as appearance went, the Sergeant-Major was the miniature edition of a Company Lord Almighty. A little choleric mannikin, whose legs restrained a slight tendency to relapse to the bowlegged infirmity of infancy with difficulty. The moustache was the only thing impressive about him. He could tie it up behind his ears without effort. Even more astonishing was the voice that issued from behind the Gargantuan moustache. It growled and thundered and made the Sergeant-Major, when he bellowed, seem even smaller than he was to the optical sense. When Schinzel thought, he thought in terms of the regulations and the drill book and what he expressed thereafter was as plain as a barrack yard.

The only complaint Schinzel had against the war was that it broke out just at the time when Sergeant-Major Schinzel was about to become lord and master of a provincial County court. He could not bring himself to believe in accident in this connection and regarded it as a bit of meanness on the part of the diplomats, deliberately aimed at Sergeant-Major Schinzel. He therefore referred to them in very strong language.

Corporal Schmalz did not exceed average military stature. But, standing in front of the Sergeant-Major in the orderly room, it was inevitable that he should look down on Schinzel.

"Got away with it once more, Schmalz? . . . I am glad. . . . And what's the latest? . . ."

An emotional temperament was not one of the Sergeant-Major's weaknesses, but the sight of the personal property sorted by Schmalz, gave him a shock none the less.

"Damned shame that it must always be the best. . . . Lieutenant Goebel was not in my Company. . . . But I know all about it all the same. . . . And Volunteer Biegler is one

of them, too. . . . I have got his lance-
corporal's buttons in my desk over there. . . .
I may as well send them home with the rest
of his stuff. . . . Scharf? . . . Scharf . . . Oh,
ah. . . . That surely was that drunken sot.
. . . Otherwise a fine soldier. . . ."

The Sergeant-Major drew a huge bunch of
keys from under his undress tunic and locked
up the several little packets. He stroked his
flaxen moustachios.

"You have been sent in for Sergeant,
Schmalz. . . . Have I told you that yet?
. . . The thing's going through. . . . Your
promotion may come in any day. You just
carry on as you have been doing. . . . I'll
keep my eye on you. . . ."

The announcement affected Corporal
Schmalz less profoundly than Schinzel thought
he had a right to expect.

Schmalz, of course, expressed his acknow-
ledgements to the Sergeant-Major. But the
thanks did not sound over enthusiastic.

"What's the matter with you, Schmalz?
. . . You are behaving as if I had told you
that the sun will presumably rise to-morrow
. . . as it undoubtedly will. . . . Well, well.
I can imagine what you feel like for myself.

. . . And it isn't easy to lose so many good rank and file at a blow. . . . But I too, should prefer to be in my County court than out here. . . ."

If Schinzel had once mounted the County Court record on his gramophone, it had to be played right through, no matter whether the audience had already heard it or not. Corporal Schmalz knew the record by heart. But he was careful not to interrupt Schinzel. This was a point on which the Sergeant-Major was touchy.

"And then. . . . What was I going to say? . . . Nothing doing in the way of leave. . . . Leave's stopped for all ranks for the next three weeks. . . . But if it would buck you up, Schmalz, and you'd like to have a day in town, I can let you have a movement order. . . ."

Schmalz made up his mind at once. Why not go to the town? There were a lot of things to see and hear there and a long draught of Bavarian beer was always worth having, and, if it fell in with one's mood, one could go to the estaminet "To the Seven Sisters". In front line jargon the sign acquired a rather different, more direct significance. . . .

184

The Sergeant-Major signed the permit, and an hour later Schmalz was in the little rattle-trap narrow gauge that plied four times a day to and from the line to the town.

The town was a railway base of the lines of communication and Army headquarters.

It was teeming with soldiers. Old Militia men, grizzled about the temples and beard, jostled young orderly clerks who had a papa at home, and papa in turn knew someone who was on intimate terms with a Medical Service staff officer. Young subalterns who had just squeezed through their emergency examination on leaving school, were proudly airing their brand new epaulettes. But men in the prime of life as well were striding about importantly, looking well fed and clean shaven, and sporting the most wondrous badges. A man who could claim to know his way about all these crosses and badges, stars and staff tabs, must have been a shining light of the Faculty of uniform Science. The outsiders were never quite sure; was the major of very martial aspect, officer in command of a poultry farm or officer in charge of a macaroni factory in the back area?

Sometimes a front line man appeared in the

throng and at once became the most conspicuous figure. His steel helmet on his belt, rifle slung over his shoulder, unwashed and unshaved, with all the mud of the trenches on his uniform and sometimes with a first-aid bandage, soiled with blood, the man from the trenches shouldered his way and wherever he passed, the hectic busy-ness of the L.O.C. became a masquerade.

The tense, drawn expression of his sunken face in itself appraised the tinsel smartness, the gay flummery, of the others with a contempt that was indeed unspoken but none the less eloquent for that.

Corporal Alois Schmalz, of Rengersreuth— twenty-seven houses!—had worked for six years before the war as a mechanic in the smelting works of the big city. The city was twice the size of the communication base and, judged by its traffic, considerably larger still.

It could therefore hardly have been uncouth rusticity that made the corporal hesitate to cross the station square. Before his joy ride to the town, too, he had smartened himself up a bit. The front line foot-slogger was, however, plainly manifest.

It was the force of contrast that made

Schmalz hesitate. The contrast leapt up too abruptly before his eyes and made him feel dazed.

The broad square was teeming with life. People were hurrying across it and were walking upright, as human beings are meant to walk, not perpetually doubled up and slinking so as to squeeze past Death.

Bright sunshine flooded the square and lit up the animated scene in cheerful colours.

Was it the same sun, really the same sun, that at this self-same hour was shining on the trenches and the wire, on the craters of death and the shell holes of corruption?

Schmalz drew a deep breath.

Twice twenty-four hours ago he had still been hiding in No Man's Land, in no better plight than a hare trying to find a gap in the line of beaters, and now—here.

A tricky business, life.

Corporal Schmalz strolled at his ease across the station square and turned into a broad side street. He had plenty of time, his own time, at no other man's disposal, and he could spend it as he liked.

For an hour Schmalz strolled about the street, without aim or object, only revelling in

187

the delight of being able to go where it pleased him to go and without having to throw himself flat on his face as soon as someone threw over a lever on the other side. Then he remembered a hostelry where Bavarian beer was on tap.

The public house was crammed full. They sat there, sprawling and noisy, their service caps tilted recklessly over the back of their head or over one ear, drinking, smoking and chatting to one another, or both together, or shouting to one another from their several tables.

At one table someone recognized Schmalz. A thick set infantry man, with two footcloths dependent from his ears, beckoned to him.

"Move up a bit closer, ye other foot-sloggers. . . . There must be room for the corporal at the club table. . . . Well, old chap, how goes it? . . ." The man with the footcloths dangling from his ears was the personification of cheeriness. He whistled, smacked his thigh, rubbed his hands as one who has just concluded a good bargain, and gurgled a laugh that was quite infectious.

Schmalz squeezed in between this merry

Andrew and acknowledged the beer mug set in front of him handsomely. Conversation was soon in full swing. Old memories revived and were discussed.

Only rarely did they touch on the war, and only when it served to illustrate a human touch or a quaint incident.

The privations and suffering of life in the line were hardly mentioned, and little allusion, as if by common consent, was made to personal experiences.

These men, every one of whom had braved death a hundred times, made not the least fuss about it. When they fell to boasting it always redounded to the honour of a group; of the section, of the company, of the regiment, or of the army as a whole. No one talked of himself in the singular. It was always. "At that time we. . . ."

Only warriors of the home front, who had learnt all they knew about drum fire from the official daily bulletins, developed wider points of view. The men from under drum fire kept to topics that touched them most nearly, rations and drink, smoking and sleeping, fatigues in rest billets, and their officers.

"The blighters up there get hold of a new

wheeze every day. . . . They've had a brain
wave that the rank and file are not saluting
in accordance with regulations. . . . Because
it all depends on that, you see, whether we win
or lose the war. . . . Our chief spider of a
C.O. makes us fall in for two hours a day and
march past in single file practising the salute.
. . . Damned rot!"

The whole table gave voice to its opinion
that drilling behind the line was rot. It was
not easy to penetrate the row because all of
them expressed this opinion simultaneously.

The corporal's neighbour alone preserved
silence. He blew the froth off a fresh glass of
beer, took a pull at it that would have done a
thirsty cow credit, and waited until the row
subsided. Then he blinked all round him
slyly.

"You're right enough, men of the moun-
tains. . . . But why do you make such a
beastly row about it? . . . My company falls
in every afternoon for drill. . . . I haven't
joined 'em even once. . . . They get on splen-
didly without me."

The company guffawed, and the funny man
pushed the footcloths out of his face and continued:

"Drill on top of everything else. . . . Salutin'. . . . By all means! But with my fingers to my nose, not to my cap brim. . . . The blighters simply don't know how to kill time, they're so lazy. . . . So they try to take it out of us. . . ."

Corporal Schmalz had never been addicted to drill. But it appeared to him apposite to put in a word.

"No old timer, who's been fed up with it from his service with the Colours, has any use for drill behind the line. But what about the drafts, the green stuff. . . . Is it such a blinking grievance if they have to fall in for two or three hours every day? . . . We used to have much longer spells. . . ."

The corporal's reservation was agreed to be well founded. But only for the drafts and subject to the further reservation that men over thirty should be exempt from drill behind the line, more especially when a subaltern of eighteen was in charge.

The theme, drill behind the line was therewith regarded as sufficiently exhaustively discussed to be dropped.

After a full throated song in praise of Bavarian beer and after heckling a rapacious, though licensed pedlar, conversation swung round to grub, the inexhaustible source of the liveliest debates among rank and file.

A tall gunner, rejoicing in a curiosity of a nose—it was not larger than an electric bell push—held forth:

" Last week they gave us an issue of herrings for tea. . . . Did they stink by any chance? . . . Enough to make an Esquimaux cat . . . no one even touched the muck. . . . When it got dark the herrings were collected . . . we bored holes in their tails and threaded the herrings on a string. . . . By morning, three of these herring garlands were in position, one hanging over the O.C.'s billets, one over the sergeant-major's and one over the quarter bloke's."

The laughter that greeted this unusual tribute was loud and hearty.

But through all the jokes and tomfoolery trotted out on the subject of rations, there ran an undercurrent of indignation and resentment that applied more especially to the differentiation made between the rations for the other ranks and officers.

On the subject of medals and decorations the views expressed were quite contrary to regulations. The corporal's neighbour broached the topic.

"Well, there was a time when the Iron Cross Class I stood for something. . . . But that's a long time ago. . . . Nowadays every slinker in the Commissariat is running about with it. . . . For one man who has honestly earned it, there are ten profiteers, comfortably tucked away in the back areas and shirking for good. Of course, I shirk myself if it can be worked. . . . But I don't expect a medal for doing it. . . ."

The table agreed unanimously and encouraged the speaker to enlarge.

"Of course I shirk whenever I can. . . . But I've never reported sick when we were under orders for the line. . . . But I want to be left alone out of the line and want to have decent grub. . . . They can leave out all that eyewash of honour and glory. . . . We were in the line for ten days on the Somme and were to be relieved. Then what does our G.O.C., the old dotard, gone at the knees, do? . . . He reports that the division can carry on in line for another three days. . . . And why does he so report. . . . Because he hasn't got the *Pour le Mérite* to hang round his neck. . . . He got it all right then. . . . Our company came out forty-four strong out of a rifle strength of nearly two hundred. . . . It was much the same thing throughout the division. . . ."

Examples of this ambition, gratified at the expense of the troops, were contributed by further speakers. But they did not in any way depress the spirits of the gathering. On the contrary, it became more hilarious with every glass.

Their faces were glowing, their heads hot, their eyes shone with the joy of life and that devil-may-care zest to play the world a trick whether it likes it or not. Not only men at the table at which Schmalz was sitting, the whole company was on its feet. One or two were already tuning up their voices in spite of the early hour of the afternoon.

An accordion gave impulse to this mood. Someone was playing in a corner. Squeaking and whining soulfully, it snorted in louder bursts as the empty bellows filled again.

At first only a few joined in, but the whole gathering was soon singing:

Just pour us out some Bavarian beer
We want to make glad on Bavarian cheer.

This hint was taken by mine host and his two sturdy, flaxen-haired daughters and carried into effect to the best of their ability. A general toasting of good fellowship from table to table drew the merry crowd into closer unison. And because, when mouth and stomach, nose and eyes are taking their pleasure, sentiment urges its claim. The accordion played a soulful soldier ditty:

> *In the garden's darkling arbour*
> *Where the moonlight falls serener*
> *Sat a huntsman in the arbour*
> *With his true love which was Lena.*

> .   .   .   .   .

> *" Darling Lena," spake he softly,*
> *" Lena, from thy tears refrain,*
> *In a year when roses blossom,*
> *I shall be with thee again."*

The ballad has thirty-four stanzas. The singer did not skip a single one of them.

Corporal Schmalz was blissfully happy. He drank glass after glass without undue haste and joined in the singing wholeheartedly. While singing, he closed his eyes until only a narrow slit was left open. A reserved man by nature, he dreaded nothing more than to display his feelings. He would not have been able to sing a note by himself, but in the company of kindred spirits, he gave voice to his surplus sensibility. He watched like a lynx to make sure that nothing Lena and her huntsman had to say to one another was excised. Nor did he jib when the tone, and more especially the text of the songs, became coarser and more direct.

In Hamburg there's a handsome house
  (All for eleven pence!)
And a dark brown nun in a stylish blouse
  (All for eleven pence).
Vallerali—Vallerala
  (All for eleven pence).

The doggerel was bellowed by all of them, loudest of all by Corporal Schmalz, who winked knowingly at the elder of the two girls.

The walls of the inn were privileged to hear many other beautiful and strange ditties which must have given them cause for astonishment that afternoon and evening. The last gleam of sunlight slid across the wall like a genial smile.

Corporal Schmalz had drunk as it becomes a man. If, later on, one or two witnesses swore that Schmalz was blind drunk, they did it only to get the corporal out of trouble. He really was only in that state of exaltation that sees the world in its rosiest light when he thought of the return journey and took his departure.

The leave taking was hearty and noisy.

For the first two or three steps Schmalz swayed, but that was due to the transition from the stuffiness of the inn to the fresh air. He pulled himself together at once and walked peaceably to the station. He was whistling and humming quietly to himself and was perfectly content with his excursion into the life of common humanity. In his thoughts he entered the day on the register of his pleasantest recollections.

There was a big crowd on the platform. A troop train must have arrived shortly before. The men were standing about in bigger and smaller groups and putting their heads together. There was a good deal of cursing and swearing with an undercurrent of dull resentment. In between, whistles shrilled.

Corporal Schmalz turned to the man nearest to him and inquired what it was all about. The troop train had taken nine days on the journey and the men had had their last meal sixty hours ago. The tired and hungry men had been looking forward to this destination, but had been kept hanging about the station for three hours without any sign of bite or sup. They were in a nasty temper and made no secret of it.

A voice rose to a bark and a rotund major shot up and down the platform. He roared at every man who crossed his path. At first sight the man looked almost easy going until he opened his mouth. Then it emitted that tone of voice which the private hates most of all. This tub of an officer was of the familiar type that tries to effect everything by the chest note of self-convinced authority.

The officer had just been roaring lustily at a young soldier, who reminded Schmalz—he never knew why—of Biegler, the volunteer. The corporal felt his scalp becoming prickly. He turned round and walked up the platform.

Then the major rushed at Schmalz like a bull, maddened by horse flies, and shouted at him :

"What's the fellow loafing about here for. . . . A corporal, too. . . . You go to the devil or, I'll help. . . ."

What ensued then was never wholly elucidated.

The Blow in the Face

The major, struck by a violent blow in the face, staggered back and, bleeding from nose and mouth, snatched at his holster. Before he could draw his automatic, a kick shot him between the rails.

Quietly, without moving from the spot, a N.C.O. of medium height stood on the platform and waited for the guard.

An hour later, Corporal Schmalz was under arrest. He had offered no resistance to the guard.

¶ On the Turn Table.
¶ "All my Rooms give me no Joy."

THE Judge advocate, a barrister with a worried look and the rank of captain, turned over his papers jerkily and picked out a file. He balanced the blue covers in his left hand and then opened them.

For the eighth time the Court Martial officer buried himself in the case of Alois Schmalz, Corporal of a Machine-gun Company, under arrest for breach of discipline before assembled troops and bodily violence to a superior officer.

"This business is going to drive me crazy," muttered the Judge advocate. " Splendid reports from every quarter. . . . Irreproachable conduct. . . . Up to that evening. . . . An excellent soldier. . . . What is the man playing at. . . . True, he had been in a public-house for seven or eight hours. . . . But nothing at all happened there. . . . Incomprehensible . . . quite incomprehensible. . . . Let's have another look at his civilian papers. . . . Small farmer's son of Rengersreuth, then

mechanic . . . no record of any previous conviction in civil life. . . . Had socialist lean-
ings. . . . H'm. . . . H'm. . . . That perhaps accounts for it. . . . Rot! . . . In that
case there wouldn't be a single superior officer
who hadn't been thrashed. . . ."

The Judge advocate lit a cigar, crossed his
hands behind his back, and tip-toed up and
down his office. The case was obviously wor-
rying him. He pressed a bell. The orderly
stood to attention at the door.

"The prisoner Schmalz to be brought
here."

During the week which he had spent under
close arrest, Alois Schmalz had not changed.
He had preserved his quiet reserved manner.

The Judge advocate raised his spectacles and
studied the delinquent with his short-sighted
eyes.

"Now, Schmalz, just tell me exactly what
really happened. . . . Think it over carefully
and tell me everything there is to be told. . . ."

Schmalz began his report with his journey
to town. He described the hours spent in the
inn in full detail and without mock modesty
made no secret of the enjoyment it had af-
forded him.

The Judge advocate listened attentively. Then he intervened with a question:

"One minute. . . . You were enjoying yourself. . . . I can quite understand that. . . . But tell me, was there not a good deal of abuse going about, about the officers and that sort of thing. . . . You know what I mean?"

Schmalz had never lacked intelligence. He was well aware at what this question was directed.

"We simply discussed things that are being discussed everywhere. . . . Most of it I didn't listen to. . . . I was looking forward to the singing."

Conscientiously, Schmalz enumerated the songs that had been sung and, rather startled, the lawyer made a note of them. He had hitherto believed that the "Wacht am Rhein" and "Birdies in the Wood" comprised the repertory of the German Army.

"And there was a young soldier, too. . . . He was wearing spectacles. . . . When the major shouted at him, I suddenly thought of Biegler. . . ."

A motion of the lawyer's hand interrupted Schmalz.

" Biegler? . . . Who's Biegler? . . . First time you've ever mentioned the name. . . ."

In a few curt sentences, Schmalz gave the information desired.

" I had brought him in the night before. And the youngster was like him in looks. . . . Then when the major rushed at me and called me a fellow, it just happened. . . . I don't know how myself. . . ."

During the whole of the story about Biegler, the Judge advocate had been taking notes. He asked one or two further questions and then Schmalz was taken away.

He put down his cigar; it had gone out in the course of the examination. The Judge advocate lit it and continued pacing up and down the room. He began talking to himself.

" The whole case is becoming more and more maddening. . . . This Biegler business only complicates it a bit more. . . . I can understand it all right. . . . In the course of the previous night he brings in a buried comrade. . . . Splendid fellow, by the way, this man Schmalz. . . . Very good: he brings him in and in this ruction he meets another man who is the image of his dead comrade. . . . But how am I to drag this into my state-

203

ment of facts in such a way as to make the horny-headed mules of a Court Martial understand it? . . . It's the very devil of a case."

The lawyer's paces grew shorter and more restless. He puffed his cigar absent-mindedly and scrubbed his chin and nose.

Suddenly his puckered face relaxed. The lawyer went to his desk, straightened out the file and drafted a minute recommending that the prisoner Schmalz undergo medical examination in regard to his mental condition and be kept under observation to this end in an appropriate institution.

"The only chance of saving that man from the worst," he muttered to himself. He rammed his cap on his head with a sigh and left the room with an expression of discontent.

The next morning a corpulent medical officer on the staff was tapping Corporal Schmalz all over, looking into his mouth, nose, ears and eyes and circled round him three times. He asked questions about his parents and grandparents, manifested a lively interest in his father's and grandfather's thirstiness and was ill content with the information received. This found its expression in an irritable grunt.

In addition to an impressive paunch, Dr.

Frucht could boast of a really resplendent bald head. He tapped this bald area at the approximate site of the nape of a neck that had vanished long ago.

"Haven't you got pains at this spot at times?" he asked.

When Schmalz said no, the sausage-like fingers of the staff physician slipped over the polished dome to the lower base of the back of the neck. Here, in Dr. Frucht's case, three handsome bulges protruded and surmounted the collar of his tunic. To these three folds in the back of his neck, Dr. Frucht owed his startling nickname, "the Trinity doctor".

"But here you surely must feel something. . . . A strain or a tickle . . ." prompted Dr. Frucht zealously.

Schmalz could not see why he was bound to feel something and again answered with a decided "No, sir."

Dr. Frucht gazed in consternation into the ambient air with the manner of a man who had reached the limit of his craft, scratched the bacon on the back of his neck and then growled angrily: "That'll do. . . . Take the man away."

The staff physician twiddled the penholder in his fingers, tapped the palm of his left hand with it and minuted his opinion. He smacked his lips like a gourmet during the operation and read through his minute for a second time:

"Something must be wrong with the man. . . . Only it cannot be stated at first glance what it is. . . . He does not look like a shammer. . . . Rather the contrary. . . . To be kept under observation for six weeks. . . ."

Dr. Frucht attached his medical confirmation to the Judge advocate's minute, applying for the observation of the aforesaid Schmalz and reverted to the further business of the day.

Ten days after the incident at the railway station, Corporal Schmalz was escorted to the observation station.

In soldier's parlance this establishment was known by the significant name of "the turn-table".

It was a grey, gloomy building. The dark staircases and the long, white-washed corridors confirmed the impression of sombreness and distaste. The whole house had a sour smell.

This smell struck Corporal Schmalz at the out-
set and stirred violent dislike in him.

A shrivelled little man, of a yellow com-
plexion like a case of jaundice, was the officer
in charge of this institution. Eyes, sharp as
a weasel's, flickered unrestfully in the yellow
face.

Dr. Gurkner read the Schmalz file right
through and smiled maliciously at the opinion
of his colleague, Dr. Frucht. What did that
man know about simulants? They had been
brought to him, the well-known specialist, by
the gross, but the artful dodger who could take
Dr. Gurkner in had yet to be born. No indication of shamming! What did he mean by
no indication?

Every human being is a born simulant and
no indication? That would be contrary to the
laws of nature.

Whenever Corporal Schmalz's eyes rested
on the little doctor he could not help, throughout the whole examination, thinking of a half-
ripe pumpkin. This mannikin must be fash-
ioned out of one of these pumpkins.

What was the doctor after? He sprang the
most insidious questions and in a twinkling
twisted the answers Schmalz gave clearly and

definitely and made a face as one who should say, " Well . . . who was the first to invent gunpowder now? "

For over two hours Dr. Gurkner pried and probed about Schmalz with penetrating words and eyes without discovering a trace of neurosis. He almost boiled over at the quiet, assured manner of the N.C.O. and finally almost flung Schmalz out of the room.

Was it possible that his colleague, Dr. Frucht, might be right after all? That could not be and must not be. The theory that all men are shammers would in this case not hold water. Hence Dr. Gurkner came to the conclusion: this man Schmalz is a born simulant and a dangerous one to boot.

This was the conclusion Dr. Gurkner reached after every examination and in every case. Why should he make an exception in Schmalz's favour? The methods of treatment in the establishment were based on this axiom. A man could do or leave undone what he pleased, the contrary of what he did or left undone was regarded as his normal state of mind and real motive.

The section under which Schmalz was placed was under the supervision of a silent
208

warder who stole about day and night in felt slippers. The man had green eyes and a malignant expression on his clean-shaven face. When he contrived to make the effort to talk at all, he spoke in a sickly sweet, plaintive voice. On the other hand, the warder watched his charges for hours through secretly contrived spy holes, counted every step they took, made an entry every time they scratched their heads, in a bulging pocket book and was the theory of the director of the institution become flesh in practice.

Corporal Schmalz had the haziest notion of the workings of the turn-table and abstained from thinking about it too much. But from the first moment of his transference thither, the house and everything connected with it was hateful to him. He felt he was being watched, before long could not stand the warder's green eyes, and began to become confused and not sure of himself. Like all simple people, Schmalz had a deep-seated dread of everything connected with mental infirmity.

The first night Schmalz hardly closed his eyes and went on listening to the uncanny noises all about him. One man suddenly shrieked hideously, another fell in with an inhuman howl, others groaned and panted, and amid it all there was something flapping dully and continuously.

Of the sixty inmates of the institution the majority had been sent in for observation, but there were one or two cases as well whose condition did not leave room for doubt.

As early as the second day, Schmalz made the acquaintance of a patient who believed himself to be the Pope. A big, strong man, he kept his arms spread out in blessing and mumbled prayers and benedictions. Another had lost his reason after being buried. When he was not strapped to the bed, he was crawling all over the ward on all fours looking for a hole through which to escape. He sobbed and cried like an infant while doing so.

A third sang incessantly, "There's no nobler death in the world," only these seven words over and over again and only broke off, to crow and flap his arms as a cock flaps its wings.

Not all the inmates of the turn-table had succumbed mentally to the war and its impressions to the same degree. There were some simply weak-minded, others suffering from St.

Vitus' dance or asphasia and there were also some mild melancholics who timidly avoided every human being and, for days together hardly uttered a sound.

But whether one thing or the other: the misery of it cried to heaven and Corporal Alois Schmalz of Rengersreuth woke every morning dripping with perspiration, if indeed he had closed his eyes at all.

Three days on the turn-table sufficed to make Corporal Schmalz a changed man. He looked pale, slouching in movement and was easily startled, and without cause. Since he ate little and was sleeping badly, they attributed the change to these conditions.

In spite of all his spying and note-taking the warder was not able to spy into the human brain.

In this brain, imperceptibly from without, the fate of Corporal Schmalz was working itself out.

The corporal had always been taciturn and reserved. Yet his quiet ways had never cast a gloom over others because, underneath this unresponsiveness of manner, there was a quiet serenity, an innate delight in real and simple life. And now Schmalz became aware to his alarm, that this serenity was failing him like the gleam of a mirror going blind.

Corporal Schmalz used to sit for hours at his table now, brooding. His thoughts were, like himself, simple, uncomplicated, honest, and deepseated.

He had by this time been on active service for forty-one months, twice wounded, and signalled out for distinction four times. He had been called up as a simple private, within a year he had got his lance's buttons, within two years and a half his corporal's stripe. He was about to be promoted full sergeant and vice warrant officer.

At this point the corporal's thoughts began to stray. The bowlegged sergeant-major was suddenly standing in the room and cursing in his voice of thunder. Schmalz saw him quite distinctly and heard his rough dressing down word for word.

"What did I tell you at the time, Schmalz, when you wanted to go to town. . . . You have been sent in for sergeant. The promotion may come along any day. . . . That's what I said. . . . And, further, you just carry on as you have been doing. . . . Or didn't I say that? . . . And what do you do? . . . Go into town, get drunk, and strike and kick your superior officer. . . . What sort of figure do I, Sergeant-Major Schinzel, cut now? . . . Didn't I recommend you for your step? . . . That sort of thing makes one fed up with the whole job. . . . But once I'm back at my County Court. . . ."

A very slow smile lit up the corporal's face that died out in the corners of his mouth.

Old cantankerous ramrod! But he had always meant well by Corporal Schmalz.

To have to face the Sergeant-Major again. . . . No. . . . No! . . . His brooding thoughts groped their way back into the past.

"This promotion's," so brooding set in afresh, "a very stupid business. . . . The warrant officer's sword would have looked all right. . . . None of the Rengersreuth conscripts, if he were a foot-slogger, had worn a commissioned officer's sword. . . ."

The corporal's brow was puckered in deep furrows.

"What's going to happen next? . . . They'll keep you here on the turn-table for six weeks. . . . By the end of six weeks you will undoubtedly be mad, Alois. . . . And if you aren't, what then? . . ."

213

The vision of a full-dress court-martial appeared before his eyes. They would sit in a dark court-room where the gas is kept burning all day long. The members will sit at a long table, among them perhaps, one or other who knows Corporal Schmalz. Then proceedings would begin. The presiding officer would ask: "What made you do it, prisoner?"

Corporal Schmalz had composed a long speech in reply to this question and rehearsed the speech to himself:

"Sir, if I am to answer the question of the officer presiding I have to ask leave of the Court to be allowed to relate of the antecedent incidents. . . . During the night before that for which I am under arrest occurred, I was in the line. . . . I was looking for Pillbox 17 with three pioneers. . . . We succeeded in finding the strong point. But my comrades-in-arms were all dead . . . Everyone in the strong point was suffocated. . . . Lieutenant Goebel had shot himself. . . . Among my comrades was a young volunteer, an artist. His name was Biegler. . . . But we used to call him the Pillbox infant and were very fond of him. . . . Well, when the major was finding fault on the platform, he came up to a

young private who was wearing spectacles.
. . . This private reminded me so much of
Biegler. . . . I had dug Biegler out only
twenty-four hours before. . . . He was looking quite peaceful and his face was not a bit
livid. . . . It flashed through my head : Sup-
posing that had happened to Biegler, for a
man to be shouting at him like that, when he
died such a painful death. . . . Then I turned
and went away not to see and hear anything
more. . . . The officer ran after me and called
me a fellow. . . . It was like a blow in
Biegler's dead face. . . . And then everything
happened as it did. . . ."

Corporal Schmalz had thought out this
speech, but he shook his head in hesitation the
more he considered its several pleas.

Who would believe his story about Biegler?
And could the Court believe it? On the faces
of the members of the Court there was sure to
be an expression indicating that they regarded
this reference to Biegler as a fairy story, or a
rotten excuse. What was the good of all this
talk. He could tell the Court what he liked.
He was sure of his three years. Perhaps they
would send him to a military fortress, instead
of to gaol because there was no previous crime

on record against him. But what was gained by that?

Corporal Schmalz compressed his lips tightly.

Three years. . . . That meant three times three hundred and sixty-five days, in all—one thousand and ninety-five days. Was he, a man who had never been under lock and key for an hour to serve this eternity of a sentence?

For half an hour Schmalz stared at a spot in the corner of his room. A hook was made fast there, a little over a man's height.

Then, quite suddenly, a mood of wild exhilaration overtook him. He saw himself back in the inn where he had spent his last cheery hours.

Without really knowing he was so doing or intending to do it, Corporal Schmalz whistled and sang, cracked his fingers and smacked his thighs.

Behind the door stood the lurking warder writing in his notebook. He had already filled several pages with scribbled notes and was pleased with his work. Dr. Gurkner was sure to commend him and glean hints for the further treatment of the dangerous simulant, Schmalz, from his observations.

But by reason of the excess of his antici-
pated satisfaction at the commendation expected, the warder overlooked one trifle in the
corporal's behaviour. It quite escaped him
that Schmalz, after whistling and singing himself to a standstill, remained standing in the
middle of the room, took off his neckcloth,
and clasped both hands round his neck. Nor
did the warder note the glance towards the
hook.

On the following morning the warder
knocked in vain at Corporal Schmalz's door.
The room was locked from the inside, the key-
hole blinded and not a sound was to be heard.

The door was burst open. The warder
staggered back.

Corporal Alois Schmalz of Rengersreuth
was dangling from the hook in the corner.

When the warder reported the news to Dr.
Gurkner, instead of the commendation awaited
the day before, there was a devil of a hullabaloo.

Hurriedly the little doctor stumped into the
room and glared at the body like a man de-
mented. All doubt was ruled out and so was
any question of shamming.

The dead man's tongue protruded from be-

217

tween his teeth and seemed to be extended against something or other.

On the table were the corporal's watch, wallet, identity disc and correspondence, all tidily arranged round a big piece of paper.

It was a sheet of brown packing paper. This sheet held half a dozen names of Corporal Schmalz's comrades-in-arms and this verse from an old song:

> *" My cottage's neat and small*
> *But I am in my cot alone*
> *And all my rooms*
> *Give me no joy*
> *'Cos I'm in my cottage alone."*

The report of the Director of the Institute stated that Corporal Alois Schmalz, transferred for the purposes of observation had, on the fourth day of his domicile in the institute, voluntarily set a term to his life by hanging. Presumably in an access of melancholia.

The Judge advocate drew out the file in *re* Schmalz, stroked his chin reflectively before dipping his pen in the ink, and wrote conclusively under the official statement of case: " Voided by reason of decease."

Sergeant-Major Schinzel spoke the last epilogue. When he took custody of the dead man's personal effects, he produced the huge bunch of keys from under his undress tunic and said very loudly and distinctly:

" Damned folly."

It has never transpired whether Schinzel was apostrophizing the case of Corporal Alois Schmalz alone, or the war in general.

This is the story of the Pillbox, embodying the fate of strong point 17 and of its leader, Corporal Alois Schmalz of Rengersreuth, holding the distinction of the medal for Valour and the two Iron Crosses which a loyaler breast has never borne.

Spring once again is casting its sheen of green over the hillsides round Rengersreuth as over that flat plain, far to the Westward, where once Death's strong point used to stand.

The same blossoms, cradled in the same breeze, twine round the grey remnants of the Pillbox as round the plinth of Rengersreuth's War Memorial.

This memorial stands half-way above the houses and records seven names.

They do not include the name of Corporal Alois Schmalz.

This is a plain indication that henceforward Rengersreuth is not minded to make itself conspicuous in the history of the world.